THE SIN COMMANDMENTS

A Regency Historical Romance
A Sin Like Flynn novella

By Kathryn Le Veque

Not content to follow the family business, Rory Flynn is embittered by the Sinning Flynns' reputation as a wildly wealthy family from Irish stock, hated by the *ton* but accepted because of their links to the crown.

The worst offender against his family is none other than the man Rory's mother jilted those years ago, the Earl of Exford. He's never forgiven Lady Amy for her offense against him even though he managed to marry well. Knowing the earl and his daughters will be at the Stag Ball, Rory is determined to compromise one of them so they will be forced to wed. But what he didn't count on was a chance encounter with a sweet, beautiful woman who pulls him off his quest.

As he goes in pursuit of Lady Edith "Edie" Rhodes, Rory finds himself entrenched in a world where secrets are darker than his own and sins are something that can never be forgotten… but can be forgiven.

Will Edie forgive him his family's past – or can Rory forgive her for withholding hers?

The Sin Commandments isn't just a title…

It's the code that Rory Flynn lives by, a code that has taken a lifetime to compile. Rory has built his life on the backbone of his family, becoming a greater smuggler, a bigger rake, and the most notorious brother. The code of conduct he lives by is something that shapes his life and on the night of the Duke of Savernake's Stag Ball, it's a code he intends to use.

Every word of it.

But codes change.

And so do men.

Welcome to Rory and Edie's story.

PROLOGUE

May 1811
Behind The Hungry Horse Tavern

H E'D SAID HE loved her and that made this encounter a holy thing, because if God was love, then Myles Forrester was possessed by the holy trinity.

When he'd said he loved her, she had believed him.

Now, it was time for her to prove her love to him.

It had been soft and dark and quiet in the livery behind The Hungry Horse, an ancient tavern near her home and easy for her to reach. That's where he'd told her to meet him and meet him she did.

For a goodly dose of the holy trinity.

It hadn't been easy, however. Her parents were aware when it came to her adoration for the older, married man who had taken such a fancy to her. He had wealth, so he wasn't after her money. He simply wanted a young, nubile body in his bed and that's exactly what he was pursuing.

Her young and nubile body.

His wife didn't understand him. Myles had told her that a thousand times. She was the mothering type who, after having children, ignored her husband completely.

At least, that's what he'd said…

He needed what only the young and nubile could provide. All he could speak of was his longing for her and she'd declared her longing for him. He'd come for her now and would make everything right between them, as he'd promised. He'd divorce his wife, just for her. Divorces were practically unheard of, but for her, he would risk the shame and expense of it.

He'd sworn this.

But first, he needed a demonstration of her love for him so he knew that he was doing the right thing.

So, she met him in the livery behind The Hungry Horse Tavern. It had been very late at night, when her entire family had been asleep, and it had been a simple thing to slip out and come into town. He'd come to her in the livery, smelling of wine because he'd been drinking all evening.

At first, he had been gentle, and their embraces had been innocent. But that innocence was short-lived when he pinned her against the stable wall and his mouth began to wander, his tongue tasting every bit of flesh from the shoulders up. She'd resisted at first, but he had ignored her resistance as he continued to speak of his love for her. Of her love for him.

If you love me, you will prove it, he'd said.

His tenderness soon turned rough.

Now that he had her where he wanted her, he wasn't going to waste any time.

With the idea that she needed to prove her love for him, her uncertainty faded. If she loved him so much, then surely they were doing the right thing. As the horses around them shifted and snorted, he grasped her by both arms and pulled her down onto the cold, dirty straw at their feet.

Forcing her onto her back, he began fumbling with the bottom of her cotton gown. The cloak was in the way and he tossed it aside. He was a big man and his old, sweaty body was heavy atop her, squeezing the breath from her, and her hesitation returned. Her eyes remained open, darting around frantically, as he kissed her with a sloppy mouth.

The skirt of her dress was pushed up, past her knees as he tried to expose her soft, white body beneath him. He grunted and gasped and sweated on her as his hands continued to yank up the fabric He couldn't pull it any further, so his hand came in from the top of her bodice.

Once he touched her bosom, she realized exactly what he was intending.

That's where the progression stopped.

"Myles," she finally hissed, pushing his hand away and pulling her clothing back down. "We cannot do… *this.*"

"Why not, my dearest?"

With the last shred of willpower, she pushed him away and sat up. "Must I explain this to you, truly?" she said. "Because if we continue along this path, it will be my ruin and the ruin of my family. You cannot expect me to participate in my own destruction this way."

He was panting. "But if you love me…"

"If you love *me* you would not demand such a thing."

He looked at her as if she'd gravely wounded him with her words. "I do, Edie," he breathed. "You know I love you."

"Then we will pursue a respectable relationship *after* you have divorced your wife."

"But…"

"I trust that you will do the right thing, Myles," she said in a clipped tone. "If you love me, then you will not ask me to do things that respectable ladies don't do."

His eyes glittered in the darkness, reflecting the distant light from the gas lamps in the livery yard. After a moment, she heard him sigh heavily.

"Do you mean I cannot touch you unless I have divorced my wife?" he asked, his tone far different from the breathy tone he'd been using. "Is that fair, Edie?"

"It is not only fair, it is necessary," she said. "Why would you take issue with this? You have told me that you intend to divorce your wife. That is why I met you here tonight. Did I misunderstand you?"

He paused. Perhaps it was because he thought he could get away with something tonight, something to satisfy him and ruin her for life. He was very fond of her, but mostly because she was pretty and compliant.

At least, she used to be.

But tonight, she was taking something of a stand.

"You did not misunderstand me," he said, sounding vastly disappointed. "But I must ask – if you did not intend to demonstrate your love for me, why did you answer my summons?"

Edie could feel the warmth that had been so recent between them drain away. It was a cold question looking for a cold answer. She backed away from him and stood up, brushing the straw from her skirt.

"Because I thought you had something to tell me," she said. "Good news."

"Is the news that I love you not enough?"

"It will mean more when your actions prove it."

Myles wasn't happy in the least. His entire face changed, his features taut and bordering on rage. But he simply nodded, an insincere gesture, and stood up, brushing the chaff off his fine breeches.

"Will you at least let me ply you with wine?" he asked.

Edie shook her head. "No," she said. "There might be someone inside who will recognize me. I will return home, Myles. I will wait for news of your divorce there."

With that, she turned on her heel, making her way back into the cold night, walking away from a man she thought she loved. She truly did. But Myles, so far, had been long on promises and short on action.

But still, Edie held out hope.

Tonight, she left with a wounded heart, but at least her innocence was intact.

And she intended to keep it that way.

God help her, it was the beginning of the downfall of Edie Rhodes.

CHAPTER ONE

*"Thou shalt seek vengeance… in the most satisfying
way possible…"*
Sin Commandment #1

June 1813
London

THE EVENING SMELLED of dew and dampness from the River Thames, filling the air with the scent that everyone in London was privy to in the languid summer months. The day had been warm and fabric stuck to moist skin, something even the afternoon bathing and the ritual of powder couldn't remove.

But he didn't particularly care at the moment.

He was on the hunt.

The great Stag Ball would be his hunting grounds this night. He'd come for a reason. Oh, they *all* came for a reason and that reason was mostly to find spouses in the great preying lands of the ballrooms of London where the heartiest of beasts preyed upon the weak, the rich, and the beautiful – usually in that order – but for Rory Flynn, this night was different.

He had a motive in mind.

Revenge.

As the third son of the Earl of Sinbrook, Rory didn't stand a chance of inheritance. He was the most Sinning Flynn brother out of all of them – dashing, daring, and reckless in so many ways. He had glistening blond hair and flashing green eyes, a smile that could melt even the most iced maiden's heart. But most of all, he had the cunning and the ambition and the inherent sense of vengeance.

Anyone who shamed his family shamed him.

The family...

The Sinning Flynns is what Polite Society called his family, a breed descended from an Irish smuggler who had gained favor with King George III and had received an earldom as a result, much to the shock of the *ton*. The new Earl of Sinbrook had been granted a vast estate in Cornwall that was supported by the equally vast wealth the Irish smuggler had accumulated over the years.

Armed with his new title, the smuggler known as Sean Flynn had ingratiated himself to some of those in Polite Society who actually thought a Gaelic pirate added a little flair to the usually tight-lipped, upturned noses of the *ton*. One of those men had been the Duke of Savernake, a man with the mile-long name of Hugh Herbert Marmaduke Algernon Wellesbourne. His family went back centuries, back to the conquest of 1066, and he had a son, Martin, and a daughter, Amy.

It was Amy who had caused the biggest scandal of her debut Season.

Pledged to the prestigious Earl of Exford, a man named Halburton, Amy's future was set. As the most eligible young lady of the entire Season, she was much sought after by earls and viscounts and the relatives of earls and viscounts. Amy's family was wildly wealthy and any man to tame Lady Amy, with her flowing red hair and flashing dark eyes, would participate in that extreme wealth. Men who had never considered marriage before were considering Amy because of the untapped coinage she brought with her. He who controlled Amy would control some of the Savernake coffers.

But Amy had other ideas.

Sean Flynn.

In his youth, he was roguish and handsome in a way few men were. Sean had the Irish spirit in him and he was damned proud of it. In fact, he made sure that everyone around him knew exactly where he'd come from and what he was about, and sometimes that meant the Irish brogue grew stronger and the actions more exaggerated. He'd met Amy, quite by chance, when she was visiting a family friend in Cornwall and one look as they'd passed one another on the street was all it took for Sean to turn around and follow her. That had been in the afternoon. By evening, she couldn't get rid of him, nor did she want to, and by morning, he'd all but proposed marriage to her. A duke's daughter and an Irish pirate with an English title. Amy had been more than agreeable.

But there had been a complication.

And that was why Rory was here, in London.

That aforementioned vengeance.

The Earl of Exford was his target. Rich and arrogant, John Halburton had been engaged to Amy and when Amy broke off their engagement, the man made it his mission in life to ensure Amy was whispered about, spoken of, and gossiped over in the most unsavory ways possible. Men gossiped and women pointed. Rory had been far removed from it as a child. Then as he became older, attending school and finally on to Oxford, he began to have a grasp of just how much his mother had been whispered about.

Exford had a younger brother who had been an instructor at Oxford. Professor Halburton had taught Rhetoric, a class that Rory had detested, but made worse by the fact that Henry Halburton knew who Rory's mother was. He knew what she had done and whom she had married. All of that snobbery and vindictiveness was fired right at the head of Rory, in front of everyone in the class.

That was from the very first day.

At first, Rory was grimly determined to drop out of the class to save the regular punishment. But he realized that if he did that, Halburton and his vile behavior would win. With Rory and his competitive nature, that didn't sit well, so he was determined to sit in class and take every single sling and arrow that was aimed at him. When Halburton insulted him and the class laughed, he laughed right along with them. He was determined to show his classmates that the ridiculous Rhetoric professor couldn't get to him.

That was on the outside.

The inside was much different.

That kind of humiliation buried a seed inside of Rory, a seed that had grown by the day. It was the seed of vengeance. He'd even come up with the Sin Commandments, a doctrine he lived by, listing how and why and when vengeance and retribution should be achieved. Not only against Exford, but against anyone who got in his way.

Anyone who wronged him.

The months and years passed and, still, the seed of vengeance grew. It grew against Exford and his stupid brother and everything they held dear. The Flynns had taken years of abuse from a jilted suitor who had ended up marrying well, anyway. From that marriage had come two daughters.

Rory had known from the beginning how his vengeance would be sated.

Exford's daughters.

But it would be done properly. Rory may have been a smuggler at heart and a wild Irishman in his soul, but there were lines he didn't cross. Children and the weak were out of bounds. When he exacted revenge, he preferred that it be with an adult in his or her right mind, fully capable of making decisions. There would be no physical abuse; certainly, that wasn't something he condoned when it came to a woman and with men, only if he was provoked. Even the most sinningest of the Sinning Flynns had his standards.

So, he waited.

The years passed.

His grandfather, the Duke of Savernake, had a grand ball on the summer solstice every year. The Stag Ball was one of the biggest and most prestigious balls during the Season and Rory had attended every year since his mother allowed that he was old enough. He'd met countless men and women and had made countless friends. Rory was, if nothing else, likeable and personable. He had a disarming way of smiling that endeared him to most. He was generous and witty. But he'd waited year after year for Exford's daughters to come of age and attend their first Season which, of course, meant the Stag Ball. Everyone who was anyone attended.

This was that year.

So many things reflected in his mind, balls and sins and vengeance, as he sat at the gambling table he'd been attached to for the past two days. Breaks came and went, but he always returned to the table in one of the seediest gambling dens London had ever seen. The Lyon's Den, they called it, a miraculous and horrifically sordid place that was as mysterious as it was legendary. He was in the main salon of the hall where the men gambled from mysterious dealers, each with a moniker that suggested sloth or greed or gluttony. No one knew the real names of the dealers, Rory included, but that was of little consequence.

Bored with the gambling dens he owned or had a stake in, he'd only come here to win money and perhaps a winsome courtesan, one of many who prowled the place. That was typical of Rory. He was never satisfied with what he had.

Or perhaps he was simply searching for something more.

He'd know it when he found it.

Two days in this hellish place. Two days of drink and smoke and the sweet scent of perfume from both men and women. Rory had trouble sleeping, so staying up for two days was nothing to him. When he wanted to sleep, he'd force down a measure of laudanum and that would pull the veil over his eyes for a few hours at most. He was coming to think that he needed to sleep today, at least for an hour or two, because the Stag Ball was this evening and this night – this event – was what he'd been waiting for.

The time had come.

And the hunt would begin.

CHAPTER TWO

"**I**T LOOKS TERRIBLE," a young woman lamented. "This is positively ghastly the way it looks beneath my gown. Edie, what do you think?"

Edith "Edie" Rhodes eyed the silk gown that her younger sister, Matilda, was wearing. Matilda, or Tilly as she was known to the family, was making her debut this Season and tonight was the night she'd been looking forward to with great enthusiasm – the Stag Ball, given by the Duke of Savernake. It was the ball to see and be seen at this time of year, so Matilda was determined to present the perfect picture of pretty propriety.

Unfortunately, her clothing was not cooperating.

Matilda was roped into her stays within an inch of her life, holding in what her mother so sweetly termed as her "soft rolls". She was delightfully round, but she very much didn't wish to be, so she forced the poor maids to cinch her in very tightly to the point of being unable to breathe. Sausage casing was what she called it. The pale blue silk gown she was wearing showed every bump, bulge, and tie underneath the fabric and Matilda was greatly distressed.

But Edie kissed her on the cheek.

"I think you look lovely," she said, looking at her sister's reflection in the mirror. "The blue is stunning on you."

Matilda frowned as she put her hands on her belly, smoothing out the silk. "Are you certain?" she asked. "I feel as if one can see every line underneath."

Edie turned to look at her, inspecting the folds of the dress. "I think you worry too much," she said. "Silk wrinkles easily and the way you're pressing on it, you're going to damage it. Keep your hands off it and let it fall naturally. That's right. See? No lines."

She had removed her sister's hands to show her how the dress was meant to fall. It wasn't a clingy dress. But Matilda wasn't so certain, wanting to press her hands all over the dress yet trying to keep her hands away. When the maid appeared with feathers for her hair, she stopped fussing and Edie stepped away, standing near the door and smiling at her younger sister.

A more self-conscious woman had never lived.

"Well? How does she look?"

Edie turned to see her mother in the doorway. Dressed in an ivory-embroidered silk with matching slippers on her feet, she wore one of her collections of jewelry around her neck, a pearl and diamond necklace with big drop pearls. With matching earrings and her hair artfully arranged, Henrietta Rhodes looked every inch the wife of a viscount and the daughter of an earl, of which she was both. Daughter of the Earl of Ornsby and wife of Viscount Rossington, Henrietta was a handsome woman with graying, dark hair and blue eyes.

Edie resembled her down to the shape of her mouth.

"Lovely," Edie said, running a practiced eye over her sister. "If she would stop pulling at the fabric, I think we might actually make it through the night unscathed."

Henrietta watched her younger daughter try desperately not to manhandle the dress that was draped against her body.

She sighed heavily.

"Tilly," she said. "Sooner or later, your hands are going to leave prints all over that dress and those attending the ball will think that you are letting every unmarried young man in attendance rub their hands all over you and grab places that are best left unmolested. They will not believe the handprints are your own."

Matilda looked at her, horrified. "But the dress," she said, pinching at her waist. "It is so very tight."

"It is not," Henrietta said. "It is simply that you are so very round. Keep your hands off it or I'll leave you behind."

Rebuked and insulted, Matilda lowered her head. But she side-eyed her sister, standing near the doorway.

Her sister who could do no wrong when it came to presentation.

Edie was, in fact, the beauty of the family.

Willowy but shapely, Edie possessed an ethereal aura that was both strong and fragile. She looked like an angel with her blue eyes, dusky lashes, and dark hair, but it was her inner strength that set her apart from the rest.

Stubbornness, really.

Edie Rhodes did anything she damned well pleased.

As the eldest daughter of Viscount Rossington, she was rich. That was the simple truth. And what wealth – her father was quite rich from the white-faced cattle he bred in the north, not only on the Rossington estate, but on three smaller estates that he owned. One of them, Everton, was deep in the country-side and full of those cows that had made her father so rich. That's where they spent most of their time. There were also horses there, finely bred Thoroughbreds, and Edie was particularly fond of that little slice of heaven out in the wilds of South Yorkshire.

Far from the gilt halls of London's Season.

Matilda and Henrietta were quite fond of the tony London townhome in Belgravia, a gorgeous piece of architecture called Rossington House but lovingly referred to simply as Rossy. It was Matilda's first Season and her first Stag Ball, something she'd heard about for years but had never been permitted to attend.

Tonight, that changed.

Edie watched her little sister primp for her first prestigious ball in a dress that had been made by one of London's finest dressmakers. They'd come to London in late-January because preparation for the coming Season was almost busier than the Season itself. Dressmakers, shoemakers, visiting friends and the like made all of it a whirlwind.

But an exciting whirlwind.

Edie had her own reasons for being excited for this particu-lar ball, however.

"Edie." Henrietta caught her attention. "Come with me, darling. Let Tilly finish dressing, but you and I must speak."

As Henrietta blew past her, out into the corridor, Edie fol-lowed.

"What about, Mama?" she asked.

Henrietta descended the stairs that led to the main corridor downstairs, carefully gripping the banister. It would not do to step on the hem of her expensive garment and ruin it.

"The guests tonight," she said, making it down without incident. "You know how big this ball is and there will be many, many people in attendance."

"I know."

Henrietta entered the parlor. "Then you know what I am going to say."

Edie had an idea, but she didn't give herself away. That very reason for her excitement, in fact. "What, Mama?" she said innocently. "Please speak freely."

Henrietta came to a halt and turned to her daughter. "You will stay away from Myles Forrester," she said quietly. "I am not entirely certain he will be there, but he is usually a fixture at these events. If he is in attendance… stay away from him."

Edie knew that was to be the edict. She'd known it all along. This wasn't the first time her mother had brought up Myles Forrester, a taboo subject in her house yet a subject that could be broached on occasions such as this.

Edie stiffened with resistance.

"I do not know why you feel the need to say such a thing," she said. "I've not seen him in quite some time."

It wasn't exactly a lie. She hadn't seen him, but she had received a missive from him. It was why she was so excited for the Stag Ball in the first place. She hoped God wouldn't punish her for trying to mislead her mother.

"Good," Henrietta said, her gaze lingering on her daughter in a way that suggested she more than likely didn't believe her. "He is no good for you and you know that. If he is in attendance and you happen to be seen with him, people will talk and… well, you do not need that kind of gossip, Edie. Promise me that you will stay away from him."

Edie's normally easygoing nature was in danger of fracturing. "I told you I would," she said. "I think you should be more concerned with Tilly throwing herself at one of the handsome DeWolfe brothers or making a fool of herself at the midnight buffet. Truly, Mama, you have no reason to be concerned with me."

Henrietta's eyes glittered in the candlelight. "I hope not," she said. "I've had enough concern for you to last me a lifetime."

Edie didn't want to be lectured. She didn't want to hear her mother speak of things that were better left buried, things from Edie's past that hadn't seen the light of day since they had happened.

Things that didn't need to be set free in the stillness of the parlor.

"Shall I hurry Tilly?" Edie asked, turning away from her mother before she could say anything further. "We do not want to be late."

Edie was heading out of the parlor to the stairs and away from her mother and her concerns. Somewhere in the house, Edie could hear her father speaking, more than likely to his valet. Frederick Rhodes had a booming voice even when he was whispering and as she took the stairs to the second floor, she could hear her father behind her, heading into the parlor and speaking to her mother.

Anything to get away from my mother.

Truth be told, Edie had no intention of staying away from Myles Forrester. Secret messages over the years had been the extent of it, but tonight… tonight would be different. Myles' last message spoke of news, of something he was eager to tell her.

All of that hope she'd been holding on to might actually come to fruition.

If her mother found out, however, there was sure to be trouble.

CHAPTER THREE

"In all things, keep your friends close… and your enemies at a disadvantage."

Sin Commandment #3

"YOU REMEMBER THAT Rhodes girl, don't you?"

"Rhodes?"

"The daughter of Viscount Rossington."

The hackney coach was lurching over the damp road as streetlights lit the way through a marvelous sunset. Rory had left his gambling den much later than he'd expected, but it was a good thing he'd left at all. If he'd had his way, he'd still be there.

His grandfather would simply track him down and drag him out by the neck.

Therefore, he'd taken a cab home. He was looking from the window, up at the townhomes as they neared the Duke of Savernake's resplendent residence, reportedly the largest in London. Rooms and more rooms, chambers, passageways and the like comprised a gargantuan feat of engineering. His chatty companion was his closest friend and most annoying companion, a man he'd known since childhood he couldn't seem to shake, nor could he live without him.

Forbes Dinnington was that man.

"I do not think so," Rory said with disinterest. "Why bring her up? When I was asking about the guest list tonight, I meant men. Perhaps we can pull together a game."

Forbes snorted. "Your grandfather would not look favorably upon you for that," he said. "At least, the type of game you are talking about."

"The duke does not have to know."

"He knows everything."

That was true. Rory leaned back against the cab, bracing a dirty boot on the cab wall in front of him. Though the man had a stable full of his own transportation, he still took a hackney cab from time to time, especially when he knew his own driver would speak on his ungodly hours and, somehow, that would make it back to his grandfather.

Yet one more thing to keep from his all-knowing, all-seeing grandfather.

"You mean Doo?" he said, a hint of sarcasm in his tone. "Only Aidan calls him that, you know. I went through a phase when I was younger and called him Doody. Aidan was young and cried when I stole his name for our grandfather and my own father told me to stop antagonizing my little brother."

"Did you?"

Rory looked at him, smirking. "Never," he said. "That is why God gave me a little brother."

"To torment?"

"Indeed."

"But you love him, anyway."

"I suppose I do." Rory turned his attention to the townhomes moving by as the hackney team trotted down the road. "In fact, he's probably at the duke's home right now, kissing up to him like he aways does. The little bastard. Mark my words, Forbes – when the duke dies, he will find a way to give everything to Aidan that my Uncle Martin doesn't already legally own. Aidan always was the duke's favorite."

Forbes listened to him, a smile playing on his lips. "You sound bitter."

"I am."

"You have plenty, Rory. You do not need ducal funds."

Rory looked at him. "Everything I have, I've had to earn," he pointed out. "Unlike my older brothers who had some money and property given to them by both of my parents, I had nothing. And Aidan has my grandfather under his thumb, but I have no one. I never have."

"Yet you seek revenge tonight for a mother who does not love you?"

Rory lifted an eyebrow. "I never said that," he said. "She loves me. But she loves my brothers more. What I do tonight is for the Flynn name – *my* name. I do it because of that bastard at Oxford who humiliated me every chance he got. I do it for the women who will look at me tonight and whisper *Amy's son* and then look the other way. Because this is my grandfather's ball, I should be the most sought-after man there, but I will not be. Oh, people will be polite. I will dance with women. But that's where it ends."

"Then how do you expect to gain a foothold with Exford's daughters?"

Rory turned his attention to the window again. "Find the eldest one and compromise her," he said simply. "I already live with a shameful reputation. But Exford does not. Let him see how it feels for a change."

Forbes had heard this before. Too many times to count. He knew the stakes and they were high, indeed.

Higher if Rory failed.

But Rory wasn't used to failure.

"My dear Rory," he said. "You know I love you madly, but I think you bring much of this upon yourself."

Rory looked at him again, sharply. "What do you mean?"

Forbes leaned back against the side of the cab. "Because you have no regard for anything," he said simply. "Let me finish before you scold me. You are brilliant; the most brilliant man in any room you choose to enter. You have an Oxford education to prove it. You have made a fortune following in your father's footsteps, but you took it further than he ever did. Sean Flynn was clever and lucky, but you are clever and lucky and unscrupulous. You are richer than God Himself for such a young age and even as you complain that your older brothers have everything, you have even more than they do, yet you spend your life in gambling hells and racetracks and in clubs and dens that even the heartiest man would be fearful of. Yet you do it, day in and day out."

Rory was trying not to look defensive as a tidal wave of criticism and compliments came his way. "And so I do," he said. "It is my life. Let me ruin it if I want to."

"You are the most ruinous man I know," Forbes said. "But if you go after Exford's daughter, you are not only going to ruin yourself, but your entire family. Not even Savernake will be able to save you."

"I do not want to be saved."

"Then I wish you well."

Rory turned away. He knew Forbes meant well, but the man

didn't understand that he *had* to do this. He'd been planning it for so long that it was part of his very fabric.

A fabric of ruin.

After tonight, perhaps there would be no return.

"You mentioned the Rhodes girl," he muttered. "What about her?"

Forbes yawned and settled deeper against the cushioned cab set. "Oh, that," he said. "Don't you remember Edie Rhodes? She had her debut a few years ago, but she had a reputation at the time for keeping company with a married man. In fact, someone actually saw her leaving a tavern near her father's estate with this man and, after that, she disappeared for a year or two while her parents tried to repair her reputation. You don't recall that scandal?"

Rory looked at him. "I don't think so," he said. "But then again, I don't pay attention to gossip like you do. I don't seem to remember Edie Rhodes."

"You would if you had seen her," Forbes said. "She's a stunning creature."

"Truly?"

Forbes nodded. "If she's here tonight, you might have an easy conquest of it if she's as unrestrained as they say she is," he said. "Too bad, too. Her father is Viscount Rossington. There is a good deal of money there, enough to overlook any youthful indiscretions."

"Forgive and forget for a price, eh?"

"Exactly."

Rory pondered a loose woman of some means but only for a couple of moments. He turned his attention back to the street. "There are enough desperate men out there who would be willing to do that," he said. "Who else will be at the ball tonight?"

"Everyone who is anyone," Forbes snorted softly. "Several of our friends."

"Who?"

"The DeWolfe brothers," he said. "Handsome rakes, all of them. Too much competition for the women."

Rory cracked a smile. "And women like men who live dangerously," he said. "Who else?"

"Joshua Wethersfield. Remember him? With the mother that drives herself through Oxford like a madwoman?"

Rory grinned. "Of course I remember him," he said. "Joshua and I have known each other for years. A solicitor."

"A very fine one."

"I know," Rory said. "I've had need of him in the past. Anyone else I should know about?"

"The warlords," Forbes said, affectionately referring to a group of their friends who were from very old nobility. "Delohr and Russe, for example. I think DeWinter will also be there."

"It has been a long time since I've seen that bunch."

"Indeed," Forbes said. He leaned towards Rory. "If I were you, I would ask them about the rumors."

"What rumors?"

"That they have an underground fight club. Much money to be made, Rory."

That perked Rory up. "*Fight* club?" he repeated. "Why have I not heard this?"

Forbes snorted. "Because you come to these events and shut yourself up in a smoking room or in a den of gamblers," he said. "You do not mingle like you should. Dance with a few women tonight and keep your ears open. You might learn something."

Rory chuckled ironically because it was the truth. He spent

so much time pursuing his own endeavors and indulging in his own vices that he didn't keep abreast of things like he should. But tonight wasn't the night to dance with women and keep his ears open.

He had something else to do.

And he was going to do it.

CHAPTER FOUR

*"If they cannot see you coming, then they won't know
when you arrive. Be the ghost."*
Sin Commandment #4

*T*HE ARRIVAL.

It was always such a moment in the life of a young woman to arrive at the biggest ball of the year. Or her first ball. Or any ball, really. But in this case, it was different for Edie.

She was looking for someone.

He'd promised he'd be here. Myles had told her that he would be in attendance and she was desperate to see him. It had been such a long time. After their encounter in the stable and the rumors that followed in spite of their attempts to be cautious, her parents kept a very close eye on her. She went everywhere with a chaperone and that had been by design. Two years out of the public eye, away from balls and parties, waiting until the scandalous rumors died down before she was allowed to come out again.

And here she was.

Myles was somewhere, waiting.

It had been a dangerous liaison from the start.

Myles was older, a friend of her father's, in fact. That was how Edie had met him. He'd been kind to her and kinder still when she came of age. That was when the trouble started. Myles was married but his wife was a shrew and he made that clear to Edie. He had from the start. Their relationship had consisted almost entirely of secret messages and that was how she knew he would be at the Stag Ball tonight. He'd sent her a message through his valet to Edie's maid, a message that told her to meet him in the garden to the rear of the residence because he had news for her. Edie wasn't exactly sure how to get there, but she was going to find out.

The man had news and that's all she cared about.

The weather had been mild so a barouche had been ordered and Edie sat next to her sister, her gaze upon the great ducal townhome that was the very center of London society on this night. There was a massive square across from the townhome where an enormous bonfire would be lit to end the Stag Ball, and the Savernake footmen were directing traffic in and around the area.

Edie had never seen so many carriages.

There were all manner and sizes of transportation on this night as fine vehicles were directed to the steps leading up to the townhome, and women and men disembarked. Edie's barouche had to get in line to be offloaded because Henrietta didn't want to walk across mud and horse leavings and chance messing her fine silk slippers. Therefore, they had to wait their turn, affording Edie an opportunity to see all of the fashions as the nobility of London made their way up the stone steps and into the duke's townhome.

Silk, velvet, and the like seemed to be the common theme

and the color for the Season was anything pale. No vibrant colors that Edie could see, which was good considering she was wearing pink. A gorgeous pink silk frock with a crepe silk overlay that had hundreds of tiny beads embroidered into it. Her long hair was up, fashionably neat upon her head, and she smelled of the jasmine fragrance her father had purchased for her, just for this occasion.

But Myles will be the only one who smells it, she told herself.

Beside her, Matilda and their mother were chatting excitedly about all of the fine houses that were in attendance. Henrietta, in particular, seemed to be singling out all of the eligible men, and there were dozens of them. Young or old, rich or moderately rich, it didn't matter. Henrietta had her eye on them, as she had two daughters that needed husbands and the eldest one in particular.

She made no secret of that.

Though Edie had been out of circulation for a couple of years until the Forrester scandal blew over, Henrietta intended to market her daughter as a viable prospect for any proper gentleman.

Knowing this, Edie couldn't help but feel the rise of irritation in her breast. So far, it was just Henrietta and Matilda discussing the gowns and fashions, but soon it would move to men. Always men.

But Edie only had eyes for one man. "What do you think of that gown, Edie?" Henrietta asked, pointing to a yellow silk confection. "What of that color?"

Distracted from thoughts of Myles, Edie turned to look at the color on a very heavy older woman. "That is the Countess of Binbrook," she said. "I saw her at the very first ball I ever attended, the ball held in Broughton. The dogs got loose and ran across the ballroom floor."

Matilda giggled. "I remember you telling me about it," she said. "One of the dogs pissed and people were sliding all over the floor."

Edie grinned but Henrietta shushed them both. "You will not speak of such things," she said. "Look – our carriage is next. Are we ready to disembark?"

Edie craned her neck to look ahead, but she wasn't on the right side of the carriage to see the activity. Across from her, Henrietta collected her fan, preparing to step out with her head high, her jewels on display, and her eyes focused on the prize.

She knew other women would be studying her as she had been studying them.

"Then we are off," she said quietly as the carriage moved forward, guided by two footmen. More footmen were waiting to help them disembark. "Come along, ladies. We have arrived."

Henrietta was the first one off the carriage, giving her name and family name to an underbutler who was there for that very purpose. He spoke to a man standing behind him, who was writing everything down. The Stag Ball would be carefully documented, as it was every year, so the society columns would have the correct information. As Henrietta made sure to mention her father's name and title to the man doing the writing, Edie looked around at all of the people, the servants, and the splendor, all of it dazzling.

The Stag Ball was living up to its name.

But her focus was already in the garden. Edie was thinking ahead to the moment she would meet Myles, but the truth was that her date in the garden would have to wait. It wasn't as if she could simply run off. She had to remain with her mother until they entered the residence and she did, although she was quite nervous about it. She could feel herself sweating through the fabric as she followed her mother and Matilda through the entry and towards the crowded corridor that led to the receiving line and, subsequently, the ballroom.

She felt like a sheep. All she'd done for the past two years was follow her mother like a lost and lonely sheep, every place they went. No parties, no social events, but marketing or dressmaking or something else. It had become habit with her to keep her head down and follow her mother and for an independent young woman, that was a fate worse than death. But it had also been necessary to rebuild the reputation she'd shredded when she'd agreed to meet Myles Forrester in the stable.

Such was the penalty of her foolishness.

"Look there," Henrietta said, pointing to the veranda that was near the entry, facing the square. "I see Lady Criswell and her sister. I must greet them."

Henrietta rushed forward with Matilda right behind her. Edie followed, that same silly sheep again, listening to her mother engage in a lively conversation with her friends and following the women all the way to the receiving line.

But Edie couldn't even focus on what they were doing.

She needed to get to that garden.

It was a horrible conflict, knowing she had to stay with her mother, knowing this was her chance to solidify her restored reputation by behaving as a proper young lady would. She also knew that her behavior would reflect on Matilda and that was something that gave her pause. She was willing to be responsible for her own reputation, but damaging her sister's chances was something else altogether.

Therefore, she remained with her mother throughout the

introductions and the greetings and everything else that came with an event of this magnitude. She smiled at the old women who had once clucked their tongues about her, the same women who were now in approval that she'd been properly defeated and restrained. The blithe, free spirit that was once Edie Rhodes had been summarily curtailed and forced into submission. No more wandering to a livery in the middle of the night to meet a married man.

Lesson learned.

Edie was on the right side again.

Therefore, Edie knew that she had to plan her escape very carefully. No one could see her or notice that she'd gone. She would have to stay to the shadows and keep out of sight. That moment came when they'd made it past the receiving line and ended up in one of the numerous rooms that was crowded with people in conversation, all of them waiting for the dancing to commence. It was a night to see and be seen and the excitement in the air was palpable. It was, at that moment, that Edie excused herself to the ladies' room with her mother wrapped up in conversation with another gossipy matron. Henrietta gave her approval as Matilda clung to her mother.

Edie could go alone.

And she did.

The garden to the rear, his message had said. Heart pounding with excitement, Edie lost herself in the crowd, heading for the floor to ceiling doors that opened to the side of the house with the garden to the rear. Once outside in the mild June night, she moved quickly for the garden and into the bushes to make sure she wasn't seen.

಄

HE'D BEEN ROPED into the receiving line.

Unfortunately, Rory didn't have a chance to get a few hours of sleep as he'd hoped. He'd left The Lyon's Den too late and by the time he reached his grandfather's townhome, preparations were in full swing for the evening's event.

Forbes was his guest, so when the cab came to a halt, footmen were waiting. Both Rory and Forbes were hustled into the home to be met by the duke's butler, an older man by the name of Simms. Simms was quiet and efficient as always, directing Forbes to the unmarried male visitor wing, which was down on the lower level, and further directing Rory to the room he always occupied while in London.

Rory took the steps two by two, finally reaching the upper floor of the house that had the faint scent of tobacco. The duke liked to smoke and he did so without closing any doors so, over the years, the smell had permeated the very walls.

Rory found it a comforting smell.

The duke's valet, a somber man named Howard, was on his tail the moment he reached his bedroom. Howard had already helped the duke dress and since Rory's younger brother, Aidan, didn't like nor employ a valet, the man was at Rory's disposal. As Rory began to quickly undress, he eyed the valet in the mirror's reflection.

"Has my brother arrived?" he asked.

Howard nodded, his hawk-like eyes focused on laying out Rory's clothes. "He has, my lord."

"Is he in his room?"

"I am not entirely certain, my lord," Howard said. "Shall I send a servant for him?"

Rory shook his head. "Don't bother," he said. "I shall see him soon enough."

The valet finished laying out his clothing as Rory quickly bathed and shaved, something he wouldn't have normally done except he hadn't bathed in quite some time and he knew he smelled quite rancid. If the duke got a whiff of it, he'd make his displeasure known, so it was better not to stir the pot.

Rory stirred it enough without trying these days.

When he finally finished dressing and smelled like sandalwood, Howard collected his dirty clothing and carted it off, leaving Rory to finish with his hair. It was dark, with a bit of a curl, and he combed it into a fashionable arrangement. Normally, he simply ran his fingers through it and that was enough of a comb but, tonight, he wanted to make some effort so his grandfather might find something pleasing in him.

That was the hope, anyway.

Just as he was finishing, there was a knock on the door.

"Come," he said.

The panel creaked open and Aidan Flynn entered. Rory glanced at his younger brother, a sensitive soul and a man who never quite fit in with his older brothers. But Rory and Aidan were close as brothers went and they'd always gotten on, even when they disagreed.

Rory smiled weakly at his brother.

"Ah," he said. "I was told you were here. Where is Grandfather?"

"Downstairs already," Aidan said.

Rory put the comb down. "Then we had better join him before he comes up here to retrieve us."

He moved for the door but Aidan put up a hand to stop him.

"Wait," he said quietly. "I want to speak with you before you go down."

Rory came to a halt, his brother's hand on his chest. "Why?" he said. "What's amiss?"

Aidan dropped his hand. "When was the last time you saw Grandfather?"

Rory cocked his head thoughtfully. "A few months ago," he said. "Why?"

"So you've not seen him lately?"

"No. Why?"

Aidan shook his head, recalling the conversation he'd had with his grandfather and his grandfather's physician earlier in the day. A cancer, their grandfather had. The physician had confirmed it. It wasn't as if he'd been sworn to secrecy about it but, somehow, he thought their grandfather should tell Rory about his fate. That wasn't something that should come from him. But he'd had no choice and had confirmed the diagnosis when Aidan had visited the good doctor's offices.

But he wasn't sure Rory would even notice.

The man was so wrapped up in himself that he seldom saw beyond his own nose.

"He doesn't look… well," Aidan said. "He's growing older, Rory. Someday, he will die and the Stag Ball… it very well may be that it does not continue. In fact, this may be last glorious ball for all we know and although I know you had plans for Exford and his daughters, I am wondering if you would reconsider."

"Reconsider what?"

"I told you. Your plans for Exford and his daughters."

Rory's jaw tightened. "That's what I thought you meant," he said. "To that, I will say this – what I do is my business, Aidan. You have never interfered with me and I have never interfered with you, so whatever I do will not reflect upon our grandfather. Only me."

Aidan sighed heavily, as if he knew his request had been a foolish one. Rory always did what Rory wanted to do.

His irritation bloomed.

"I am asking you, for once, to think of someone other than yourself," he said. "I am asking you to think of Doo, Rory. Will you at least give the man the dignity of not causing a great scandal at his prestigious ball?"

Rory's pale eyes glittered in the weak light. "His dignity is not at stake," he said. "Exford's is. And no, I will not reconsider. I have been waiting too long for this."

That was as far as Aidan would go in pleading with his brother. The man was so selfish that no amount of begging would cause him to change his mind. Aidan knew that. Years of humiliation and shame had compounded into this night, so there was nothing that could change the direction.

Not even a dying grandfather.

Therefore, Aidan simply turned away, exiting the bedroom as Rory lingered behind. Aidan had irritated him. But the more he thought on it, he realized that there was something more behind that suggestion that this might be the last Stag Ball, at least with their grandfather at the head of it.

Something in Aidan's eyes suggested it.

Bordering on brooding, he remained in his bedroom for a short while, long enough for the receiving line to get started and for him to be a late addition. But something told him this night would be different.

There was something in the air.

A most monumental night, for all of them, was about to begin.

CHAPTER FIVE

"Time is the only true constant. Vengeance is the only true path. At some point, they will converge."
Sin Commandment #5

T HE BUSHES WERE dark.

And wet. Just a little damp and Edie struggled not to get the moisture on her gown, which would surely ruin it. How would she explain it to her mother? Therefore, she'd been forced to step out of the foliage and stay to the shadows as much as possible, terrified she would be seen and it would get back to Henrietta. The evening would be over before it started, perhaps permanently.

But then, it happened.

Myles came out of the bushes, rushing towards her in a flutter of wool and blond hair and white gloves, all of them reaching out to Edie and nearly scaring her to death.

Myles finally made his appearance.

"My darling girl," he whispered, putting his arms around her and pulling her into the shadows where the gas torchlight wouldn't reach. "You received my message. I am so glad."

Edie gladly gave herself over to his kisses. The man tasted like wine, the fine drink he consumed more than he should have, but she didn't care.

He could kiss her as much as he wanted to, wine or no wine.

"I do not have much time," she said breathlessly. "Mama and Tilly are here and if I do not rejoin them inside quickly, Mama will come looking for me."

"I know, my dearest."

"She has expressly forbidden me to see you."

"And your father?"

Edie slowed her kisses and looked at him. "He said he will kill you if he ever sees you again."

Myles slowed his kisses as well, reaching up to gently cup her face. He was tall and fair and had a tremulous way about him, as if he were always eager and trembling. It was rather endearing, something that had been useful against the army of women he'd seduced over the years. Edie was just one in a long line of many although he'd managed to keep them all fairly separate. Myles may have been married, but he wasn't reckless or stupid.

He was a man in control.

"It has been so long since I've beheld your beauty," he said, studying her face. "I'd forgotten how lovely you are."

Edie smiled, feeling encouraged by his words. "You said you had news for me," she said. "What news, Myles? What is it?"

He ran his thumbs over her cheeks. "You've been kept from me for far too long," he said. "It simply wasn't right for your parents to do that. They caged you like an animal."

Edie's smile faded somewhat. "They did what they felt was right," she said. "I cannot say I was happy about it, but they did what they felt was right to help me regain my reputation after that night at The Hungry Horse."

The light in his eyes dimmed. "I still don't know who saw us leaving the livery," he said. "Someone was clearly spying on us."

"Perhaps someone followed me. I've always thought so, though my mother would not confess."

Myles' jaw ticked faintly. "That will happen again if we are seen tonight," he said. "We must do something drastic if we are to be together, Edie."

"What do you mean?"

His features grew intense.

"I've come tonight to ask you to come with me," he said. "We'll go north, where my mother's family has property, and there is a little cottage where you will live and I will come to you when I can. I will support your every need, my dearest. What say you?"

Edie looked at him in surprise. "Go north?" she repeated. "You… you wish for me to go with you?"

He nodded eagerly, that tremulous little-boy manner coming forth. "I do," he said. "I very much do. Mrs. Forrester and the children remain at Mansfield and forever shall. My wife does not like to travel and she certainly hates the north, so we may live there as we please during the times I am able to come."

Something in Edie's expression dimmed. "Then you will not be with me, always?"

"Heavens, no," he said quickly, cupping her face and kissing her lips again. "That is impossible. But if you come with me, you will be away from your mother and father, free of their influence. They shall only know of your location if you tell them and surely you will not tell them. It will be our own paradise, my dearest. Will you come?"

His request gave Edie pause. She had a sickening feeling in

the pit of her stomach. "But… but you said that you would divorce your wife," she said. "The message you sent me said that you had news and I thought it was about your divorce. You said we could go to France and be married there, returning to England well after the scandal faded. I do not want to only be a mistress to you. I am more important than that."

"Of course you are," he insisted. "Edie, don't you understand? I choose you. I didn't choose Mrs. Forrester – my father did. But you – I choose *you*."

She dropped her hands from him. "But I want to be your wife," she said, tears stinging her eyes. "You promised, Myles."

She was backing away and he was trying to follow her, his hands on her shoulders. "My dearest darling, there are realities in life that we must face," he said. "I can never have a divorce. We must face that fact."

Edie was growing more upset. "You promised."

He threw up his hands. "I know!" he said. "I should not have. It is impossible. The expense is incredible. And the time – it could take years and years before it is granted and, even then, there is no guarantee it *would* be granted. My wife is inconsequential, Edie. She means nothing to me, to us. You mean everything. Please, my dearest… please, come with me."

More people were starting to wander into the garden now as guests arrived and began to roam the grounds. They were aware of people now within earshot and Edie moved further away from Myles, half-concealed by the bushes, eyeing him in the moonlight.

"You have made promises to me that you have not kept, Myles," she said after a moment. "This is not the first time. For argument's sake, let's say that I agree. There is no guarantee that if I go with you that you will even come to visit me."

His eyes flickered, perhaps with the realization that she was quite right. He'd never been the most dependable of men and even though their one and only encounter had been brief, she'd known him for a few years before that, as he'd been her father's friend. She knew that he'd had difficulty keeping his word. She knew that he was flighty and insincere at times. She knew that he was kind and lively and enjoyable to be around, but beneath that exterior, there was little else.

She knew.

"Do you doubt my word, then?" he said in a tone that suggested it was her problem and not his. "Is this how you treat the man you love? Edie, how can you believe the worst?"

It was simple, in truth. Though Myles was an old friend of her father's, she'd heard her father speak of him enough to know him for what he was. She supposed she'd always known it but it had never been more evident than it was at this moment.

That sick feeling was growing worse.

"I don't wish to be locked up in a cottage in the north by myself, waiting for a glimpse of you and hoping for a sweet word or a touch," she finally said. "That is not fair, Myles."

He looked gravely wounded.

"Please don't tell me that you do not trust me," he said, putting his hand over his heart. "I could not bear it if you did."

"You have broken your word to me."

"It is not my fault!"

He was starting to snap at her, a side she'd never seen of him. Gone were the warm feelings, the joy at having seen him again after so long. Now, there was only cold, hard reality between them and it wasn't pleasant. Myles wanted something and he'd beg, borrow, or steal to get it.

But Edie wasn't going to comply. It was the same merry

path he'd led her down since they'd first declared their affection for each other, a path that had only turned into near ruin for her.

But he'd come through unscathed.

"No, Myles," she said after a lengthy pause. "Understand that the only reason I came tonight is because you said you had news. And based on our previous conversations, I believed you were to tell me of your impending divorce. That is the *only* reason I came."

"But…"

She wagged a gloved finger in his face, cutting him off. "Understand that in an unguarded moment, I met you in a livery and I've spent two years of my life trying to repair that failing," she said. "Two years of spending time away from Polite Society so the rumors and gossip could recede. Time for other outrageous scandals to take place and cover up the memory of ours. Two long years of my life wasted because I listened to you when I should not have."

Myles, sensing that he was losing her, invoked the wounded expression again. "How can you think that I don't love you?" he asked. "If I am willing to provide handsomely for you and give you anything you wish, does that not profess my love for you strongly enough?"

Edie honestly wasn't sure. She was growing increasingly disillusioned and Myles' begging wasn't helping. It was only serving to inflame her. He always begged to get what he wanted, convincing her that he and his declarations of love were sincere.

But Edie was starting to disbelieve everything that came out of his mouth.

"I deserve a husband and a home and children," she said. "What you are offering is something secretive and shameful. So you will hide me away, will you? A convenience at your whim? I am to pine away in the wilds of the north, living for the very sight of you? Is that what you expect from me?"

Myles' eyes widened. "I said that I will provide most generously for you," he insisted. "You will want for nothing."

Edie sighed heavily, starting to see Myles for the very first time. A man who wanted only what *he* wanted.

To hell with what she wanted.

"You promised me that we would be together as man and wife, but now I discover that you have no intention of divorcing your wife," she said. "I risked *everything* for you, Myles. Am I not worth more than being a simple mistress? Is this what you had intended all along?"

"But you have my love, my dearest. No one can ever take that away."

Edie didn't want to hear that. A man's declaration of love was only valid if he followed through on his promises. Otherwise, it was an empty dream.

Edie was coming to realize that.

The dream was dead.

"No," she finally said. "No, I do not want to be shipped off to the wilds of the north as your convenience."

"But I adore you!"

"I will not ruin my life for you."

Their voices were starting to grow louder and Myles held up his hands, silently begging her to lower her tone. Edie glanced around nervously, hoping no one had heard the outburst, terrified her mother had realized she'd been gone overlong and was out looking for her.

"Go home, Myles," she finally said, tears stinging her eyes. "Go back to your wife and children, for I shall not be a…"

She was cut off when a man suddenly stood in their midst, a tall man with messy hair and messy clothes. He looked rather disheveled, in fact. He reeked of alcohol and body stench and Edie found herself backing away quickly, simply because he'd startled her.

But the man was looking straight at Myles.

"Are you Myles Forrester?" the man asked, his voice trembling.

Myles, unhappy with the interruption, forced a smile. "I am," he said. "How may I be of service?"

The man seemed to study him and Edie studied the man. He was trembling, his hands working into fists.

"I have been looking everywhere for you," the man finally said. "I thought you might be here tonight. The biggest ball of the season. Where else would you be? So many young women to choose from."

The smile on Myles' lips faded. "I'm afraid I do not know what you mean."

The man nodded. "You will," he said. "You see, I've been looking for you. I've followed you from town to village and back again since last summer. You are not an easy man to find, but your description is unmistakable. Tall and fair, with a big mole on your big chin. I ask shopkeepers and clergymen if they've seen you and I've been able to follow you that way."

Myles' hand flew up to his face, fingering the dark mole on the left side of his chin. "So you have found me," he said, less friendly and more suspicious. "What do you want?"

The man leaned closer. "To look you in the eyes," he said, his voice having gone from moderately friendly to threatening all in a swift breath. "You see, last summer, at a country ball in Willington, you became acquainted with my wife. Her name is

Lucy Edwards. I was away on a business venture, but I was told by servants and neighbors, gleefully I might add, that you and my wife were seen together during the ball and for three days afterwards. Months later, my wife gave birth to a baby boy."

Myles' features tightened. "Surely you do not come to…"

"Yes, I do," the man said, cutting him off rudely. "The truth of the matter is that I cannot father children, Mr. Forrester. My wife confessed that she had a liaison with you and that you are the father of her child. That is why I have followed you. A man like you must be stopped. I want to look into your eyes when you beg me for your very life."

Startled when he realized the man meant to do him harm, Myles stepped back. "Get away from me," he commanded weakly. "How did you even get in here? Get away from me or I'll call the duke's men."

But the man didn't move. He was tracking Myles with the intensity of a cat tracking a mouse. "There is a guard at the gate leading from the mews who will have a very bad headache in an hour or two," he said. "It was a matter of hitting him over the head and slipping in. But he will soon be discovered and my time is limited. I must do what I intended to do."

With that, he moved swiftly, hitting Myles in the face with a balled fist. Edie was far enough away that she didn't get caught up in the fight, but she screamed in shock and terror as the confrontation deteriorated into a vicious brawl. Others in the garden were gasping with horror and the footman just inside the door leading into the morning room, which opened onto the garden, began shouting for help.

In little time, the entire garden was in an uproar.

For several long moments, Edie simply stood there in horror, watching Myles being beaten within an inch of his life. The men had rolled close to her and she ended up being kicked in the shin, standing too close for her own good, unable to move. But men that the duke employed to keep the peace and security of his home and affairs began to flood the garden and before Edie realized what had happened, someone had grabbed her from behind and pulled her into the shadows of the foliage.

Away from the fighting and the people who were now coming to watch it.

Now, they wouldn't see her standing there in the middle of it.

When next Edie realized, she was standing in the open doorway of the duke's orangery and someone was pulling her inside. When she looked up, all she could see was a profile against the moonlight coming in through the glass walls. A strong, regal, male profile.

Evidently, her knight in shining armor.

CHAPTER SIX

"Patience is not a virtue. It is a choice."
Sin Commandment #6

RECEIVING LINES HAD never been something Rory had looked forward to.

They were long and tedious and ridiculous and most of the women simply wanted to speak with his grandfather, who was looking frail and old on this night. He could see Aidan on his grandfather's other side, hovering over the old man, and it occurred to him what Aidan may have been trying to tell him earlier in his bedroom.

Their grandfather was not a well man.

That was obvious.

Rory had only seen the man a few months ago and he'd been his usual, robust self, but over the course of those months, something had changed drastically.

And he hadn't even known.

Aidan was correct when he'd called him selfish. He *was* selfish. When he wasn't wrapped up with his business operations, he was wrapped up in himself and all of the vices that kept him going. Those addictions were like blood through his veins. The gambling, the drinking, the women were all things that kept him alive. Or perhaps not so much alive as an escape. Possibly an escape from the fact that, as he'd told Forbes, he had no one.

He never had.

An escape from himself.

As he mulled over his grandfather's physical state and the disappointment radiating from Aidan's eyes, he caught a glimpse of Forbes as the man moved through the drawing room. He was chatting with a group of other young, unmarried men and Rory identified several of them as his good friends. When he found himself wishing he was standing with them rather than in his grandfather's receiving line, he experienced an emotion that didn't normally suit him.

Guilt.

He was feeling guilty because, once again, he was thinking about himself and not his grandfather or his duty. As far as Rory was concerned, his duty was to himself, but as he watched his fragile grandfather greet his guests, that guilt grabbed at him. Would it kill him to do his duty and make his grandfather proud of him, for once?

He wasn't sure that was even possible.

"Rory?"

A voice caught his attention and he turned to see that his grandfather was now standing next to him, addressing him. But the old man was forced to turn away and greet a family of three women and their elderly father before turning to Rory once again when the group passed by.

"I'm glad that you could join me," the duke said, his eyes twinkling. "I wasn't sure you would. Better late than never, I suppose. I know how you hate these formal affairs and I wasn't sure if the lure of cards was greater."

Rory forced a smile at a man he truly loved. He just wished the feeling was reciprocated. "It's not that I hate them," he said. "It's that I think they are ridiculous. This is simply a parade of beasts, Grandfather."

The old duke laughed softly. "That is true," he said. "But a necessary parade of beasts."

"Why necessary?"

The duke shrugged. "For example, how else are marriageable people supposed to find one another?"

Rory eyed him. "Is that what this is?" he said. "A massive matchmaking event?"

"To some," the duke said. "What else would you suggest for interested and unmarried people?"

"Church," Rory said flatly. "Strolling down the street. I have no idea. But something like this… it is simply not my taste."

"It never has been. You even hated parties as a boy."

"I'm surprised you would remember that."

"I remember everything about you, Rory. I always will."

There was something more intimated in that brief statement. Something touching, almost. Rory looked at the old man more closely, seeing just how pale and gaunt he was.

He couldn't help the next question.

"Grandfather," he said slowly. "Are you feeling well?"

They were cut off when another group approached and the duke was forced to greet them. Frustrated at the interruption, Rory turned to the guests in time to see that they were the guests he'd been waiting for, the very people who had been the bane of his family's existence since the day his mother decided to marry Sean Flynn.

John Halburton in the flesh.

Caught off guard by their appearance, Rory struggled not to appear rattled. He'd hoped to see the man and his daughters before they saw him so he could map out his final plan, but that wasn't to be. Here they were, in front of him, and he watched his grandfather greet the man who had spoken so poorly of his own daughter.

Exford was sickeningly pleasant.

"It is an honor, your grace," he said to the duke. "Once again, I am thrilled and humbled to be invited to your gathering. Surely there is no more prestigious gathering in all of London."

"Thank you," the duke said, his gaze moving to the two young women next to the earl. "And these are your lovely daughters?"

Exford turned to the women. "Indeed," he said. "My daughters, Lady Rose and Lady Sarah. Ladies, this is the Duke of Savernake himself."

Rory found himself looking at the daughters and feeling a sense of disappointment but, in that same breath, he felt a sense of glee. Standing before him were two young women who were probably a little older than they should have been to have just had their debut Season and both of them, to be brutally honest, were not the most attractive of women. Sarah had blemishes on her face, neck, and chest that she'd tried to cover up with powder while Rose had close-set eyes and an enormous nose.

Women like this would be desperate for male attention.

That would work in his favor.

"Welcome, ladies," the duke said, smiling politely. He indicated Rory. "One of my grandsons, Rory Flynn. He is Amy's son, as is the other young man off to my left. That is Aidan, the youngest. Your father surely remembers my Amy."

He said it in a way that dared Exford to even hint at anything negative. Gone was the congenial old man. Before them stood a hardened old boar who suggested in just those few words that he knew exactly what Exford had been doing all these years.

Your father surely remembers my Amy.

Since the man had all but called her a whore, it was a rhetorical question. The duke's tone intimated that he was inviting Exford to say such things to his face, but Exford sensed it because he plastered a phony smile on his face and visibly demurred.

"Of course I do," he said. "I trust Lady Sinbrook is well?"

"Quite."

"Excellent."

"Good evening to you."

The conversation was over. That was Exford's cue to depart and he did, quickly, pulling his two daughters with him, but not before the eldest daughter gave Rory a rather coy expression. He smiled at her, that sly smile that had endeared him to many a maiden, before she turned away completely.

But in that gesture, Rory knew who his target would be.

His eye was on the prize.

"Imbecile," the duke muttered as Exford walked away with a tight grip on his daughters. "I wonder where his wife is."

Rory didn't know and he surely didn't care. "I would not know," he said. Then he looked at the groups that continued to filter in through the front door, resplendent in their finery. "How much longer must we stand here like baboons on display and shake the hand of every man and woman who comes in the door?"

The duke glanced at him, grinning. "Until the last one enters," he said. "The dancing cannot start until I open the ball."

"Then is there anything you wish from me before the festivities start?"

The duke was still looking off towards the ballroom. "No," he said, almost casually. "But you and your brother may assist me when I light the bonfire to end the ball."

That wasn't a hugely important task, at least in Rory's mind, but it was better than nothing. He didn't care much about this social event, as he'd indicated, but the truth was that he did care, just a little. He wanted to be included but he'd let on as much as he intended to.

"If you wish," he said, trying to sound disinterested at that point.

"I do," the duke said. But then he turned to Rory and looked the man in the face. "Until then, you have other things to do tonight, do you not?"

"Other things? Like what?"

"Like a little matter of vengeance?"

Rory's brow furrowed. "Vengeance?" he repeated. "What vengeance?"

The duke sighed heavily. "I have ears, Rory," he said. "You've made no secret of the fact that you wish to seek revenge for your mother against Exford and, truth be told, I am glad it is you. You are the wildest brother, the boldest, and the bravest. You are what I wish I could have been in my youth. You fly in the face of caution, do as you please, and have the strongest sense of family honor of all of us. Exford has been shaming your mother for more than thirty years and, in that time, you are the only Flynn brother who has had made the decision to avenge her. You are the only one courageous enough to do it. Of course

I know what your plans are. Why do you think I invited Exford this year?"

Rory tried not to look entirely shocked as he gazed at his grandfather, but when he realized the old man was on his side in all things, he couldn't help the smile that tugged at his lips. For the first time in Rory's life, he and his grandfather agreed on something.

Somehow, their relationship had unexpectedly changed.

"Then I have your permission?" he said, surprise in his voice.

The duke simply cocked an eyebrow. "I have opened the door," he said. "All you must do is step through it, if you are genuine about your intentions. Will you?"

Rory thought on his answer. It was clear that he was doing what the duke had always wanted to do but by virtue of his station, had refrained. With his daughter marrying Sean Flynn, the Savernake name had already taken a licking. It wouldn't do for the distinguished duke to seek revenge against the man Amy had jilted. In a delicate situation, the duke had taken the high road.

But that didn't mean Rory had to.

And the old duke was glad.

Glad!

"I do not intend to merely step through it," Rory said. "I intend to charge through with all my might."

A smile licked at the duke's lips. "My brave Rory," he murmured. "I shall miss you when I am gone."

"Are you going somewhere?"

The duke nodded. "Somewhere," he said vaguely. "We shall discuss it later. But in the meantime… you know what they say."

"What do they say?"

"That revenge is a dish best served cold," he said quietly. "For Amy's sake, be cold, Rory."

Rory put his hand on the old man's arm and fixed him in the eyes. He'd never felt closer to the old man than he did at this moment, as if they finally had a connection.

Even if it was a connection over revenge.

"Like ice," he whispered.

CHAPTER SEVEN

"Emotions will be your death. Feel nothing and live."
Sin Commandments #7

RORY KNEW HIS grandfather's townhome like the back of his hand.

Having spent a good deal of his later childhood here, he'd learned all of the pathways, doorways, corridors, secret passages and the like, so once he left the reception line – or, more correctly, was *allowed* to leave it – he immediately headed outside.

It was a balmy night with the gardens and grounds of the townhome lit with expensive gas lighting, fixtures with the Savernake crest on them, and it made for lovely pathways and seating areas for those who wished to venture out into the night to flirt or converse. He'd slipped out through the leather-scented library and onto a pathway that led out to the garden where it was mostly empty at this time of night because people were inside, mingling and waiting for the dancing to begin.

The scent of summer flowers filled the air like a heady wine as he made his way down the dim path. Rory wanted to single out Rose Halburton before he approached her for a dance and he didn't want to do his spying from inside the townhome. The entire south side of the structure had windows from floor to ceiling, designed to catch the sun for most of the day, and he could see every major room from the pathway.

He could also see his friends.

Along with Forbes, he could see a few of the DeWolfe brothers. There were so many of that great northern family that it wasn't unusual to see four or five at a time. They bred prolifically. He could also see Daulton DeWinter and Augustus Lara, two of the men he and Forbes had been talking about, very old families with roots deep in England's past and politics. The very men that evidently had some kind of underground fight club and the mere thought of it almost pulled Rory off of his hunt.

But not quite.

He'd get to them later.

Rory ended up on the path again with the main part of the garden straight ahead. It connected to the morning room, which wasn't usually part of a gala event, but the room was quite large and next to the library and it was being used for refreshments at the moment. He could see people inside, milling around, and thought he might have even caught a glimpse of the elusive Rose.

But something off to his right distracted him.

He could hear whispers. Ducking back into the carefully cultivated foliage, he could see a couple in the shadows. They seemed very happy to be together, holding one another as the man kissed the woman gently. At that point, they didn't have all of his attention because, from where he was standing, he could see the library and the morning room quite clearly. He was about to move positions when Rose and her willowy sister entered the morning room without their father's presence.

Rory didn't know where the earl was but he didn't care. He was on the hunt now with his prey defenseless. Rose was with her sister and he didn't exactly want an audience for what he needed to do. His only hope was if he could get the sister away from Rose so he could work his seductive magic on her.

Perhaps he needed to enlist the help of one of his friends to do that.

As he debated that possibility, he watched the young women as they met up with other young women, all of them chatting amiably from the looks of it. Now, instead of a sister to worry about, he had four more young women.

Rose was gaining a pack.

Not exactly pleased with the setback, Rory remained in the foliage and calculated his next move. But off to his right, that same loving couple was now beginning to argue. At least, the raised voices and body language suggested that. People were beginning to wander out into the moonlit garden, a breath of fresh air before the festivities began in earnest, but the couple in the shadows was becoming rather animated.

It was enough to cause Rory to look at the pair and as he did, a man came up the garden path, walked right past him, and interrupted the fighting couple. With the voices quieted down, Rory turned his attention back to the morning room and Lady Rose.

But that was only temporary.

The man who had interrupted the fighting couple abruptly threw a closed fist at the other man and the two of them went down. Shocked, Rory watched the fists fly and the legs thrash as the woman stood there and gasped. Rory's first thought was to stop the fight, but he watched the woman get kicked again, hard this time, and she stumbled back. Footmen inside the house began shouting for help and people began to swarm. The man who had thrown the first punch was now on top of his victim, his hands wrapped around the man's throat to choke him to death.

Perhaps the woman was next.

Rory had no idea why he pushed through the bushes and pulled the woman away from the fight. If two men wanted to beat each other's brains in, that was their affair, but the woman needed to be protected. In an uncharacteristic show of chivalry, he swept the woman away, through the shadowed foliage, away from the shouts that were now coming because his grandfather's men were rushing out to stop the fight. The duke had hired men on a night like this, especially with so many of the wealthy in attendance and Savernake didn't want to be blamed if anything went missing, so he always had men of protection watching out for his guests.

It was those men rushing out to stop the fight.

But Rory was halfway down the path, heading towards the front of the house. Off to his left, shrouded in the trees, was his grandfather's orangery. It was quiet and private, so he pulled the woman inside and shut the door. When she realized they were alone, she began to resist.

"Stop pulling on me," she demanded, trying to yank herself from his grip. "Unhand me at once."

Rory let go with one hand but not with the other. He had her by the wrist as she leaned towards the door of the orangery.

"Stop," he commanded quietly. "Do not go out there unless you wish to be part of a scandal that will see your family banished from the Stag Ball for generations to come. If that is what you wish, however, then by all means, go outside. I'll not stop you."

She had one hand on the door, now frozen in indecision. They could all hear the shouts as the fight was broken up, but there were more people coming out of the house to watch a completely shameful situation. She watched the people moving down the path towards the commotion, entertainment as far as they were concerned, and she took a deep breath to try and regain her composure.

The man was right.

"You… you pulled me away so I would not be caught up in it?" she finally asked.

"Yes," he said. "If two men are going to act like fools, then let them. But you should not be part of it."

She finally turned to look at him, her features partially illuminated from the distant light. "Then I should thank you," she said. "May I go now?"

He shook his head. "Wait a few moments longer," he said. "I am afraid someone may have seen you out there and they will recognize you as having been part of that mêlée. They may even think you started the fight. It is best if you stay out of sight for a little while."

"How long?"

"A half-hour or so," he said. Then he tilted his head curiously. "What happened?"

Her expression took on some uncertainty and she took another deep breath before disengaging her hand from his. "Foolishness, as you said," she said quietly, tugging at her gloves to remove them. "I've never even seen the man who started it."

"Did he say anything before he threw his fist?"

She shrugged in confusion. But then she nodded. "Something about his wife named Lucy," she said. Then her brow furrowed and as Rory watched, she sank down onto the stone bench behind her, one glove off and one glove on. "Good Christ, what have I gotten myself into? Lucy was *pregnant*?"

"Lucy the wife?"

She nodded, growing increasingly despondent. "The man said that his wife was pregnant and he could not be the father, so he accused Myles of…"

She suddenly trailed off, looking at Rory with some horror. He sat down on the bench opposite her. "Who is Myles?" he said. "Your lover?"

The woman looked as if she were about to burst into tears. In fact, after a moment, she did. "He has been promising me that we would be married," she sniffed. "All the while, he would not leave his wife. He would not even try to divorce her. He said it was too expensive."

"It is," Rory said. "He actually told you that he would divorce his wife?"

She nodded, opening the purse around her wrist and pulling forth a handkerchief. "I simply do not understand why men lie," she said, handkerchief to her nose. "No… that isn't exactly true. I think the question is why I believed him, not why he lied. Two years of being fed lies like a bird is fed breadcrumbs, little by little, leading me along a merry path and now… now, here we are. I suppose I simply never believed it until now."

"Believed what?"

She sniffled. "That his promises were as weak as his honor," she said. "That became abundantly clear tonight when he…"

She looked at Rory as if just realizing she were pouring out her entire heart to a perfect stranger. A stranger who had saved her, but a stranger nonetheless. She'd already said far more than she should have, but her emotions were running high at the moment.

She was coming to see just how big of a fool she'd really been when it came to Myles Forrester.

"Go on," Rory encouraged gently. "What happened tonight?"

The woman looked at him before smiling weakly and shaking her head. "You must think me quite ridiculous," she said. "We've not even been properly introduced."

"My name is Rory," he said without hesitation. "And you?"

She resisted for a moment but quickly gave up. She'd already told the man her damnable life story; what was left but putting her name to it?

"Edith Rhodes," she said. "I am known as Edie."

He cocked his head curiously. "Rhodes," he said, realizing he'd heard that name today when Forbes had been indulging in some gossip. "Of course. Your father is the… the…"

"Viscount Rossington."

"Of course he is," Rory said quickly, as if he'd known it all along. "I've heard the name but I am ashamed to admit we have never met. I feel as if I should have known you well before now."

For the first time that night, she smiled. "England is a big place."

"London is a small place."

She snorted. "Not so small," she said. "But the social circles are small."

He nodded. "That is quite true," he said, looking her over and remembering what Forbes had said about her. "Small and snobbish and gossipy."

Edie sighed with agreement. "Completely," she said. "What

is your family name?"

Now she had him cornered. If he'd heard about her, undoubtedly, she'd heard about him. She was a lovely woman; quite lovely, in fact, with dark hair and an angelic face. He was coming to feel a little regretful that his reputation had more than likely preceded him because he rather liked talking to her.

He'd never experienced that before.

"Flynn," he said quietly. "My grandfather is the Duke of Savernake."

As he feared, her eyes widened with surprise and she quickly stood up. "I am very sorry to have troubled you, Mr. Flynn," she said. "Please… you said that my family could be disinvited from future Stag Balls if it were known that I was involved with the brawl in the garden, but I pray you keep this to yourself and…"

Rory realized she wasn't stammering because of his reputation, but because of who he was. His family name. Therefore, he cut her off gently.

"I would not dream of telling anyone," he said, hoping to ease her. "I certainly cannot cast the first stone in the event of a scandal, so your secret is safe with me."

Edie visibly relaxed, but she was still on edge. "Everything I told you," she said with some hesitation. "I did not mean to. It simply came out."

"It sounds as if you have experienced some trouble with this Forrester man."

She nodded. "Trouble, indeed."

"Perhaps you need to speak with someone about it," Rory said. "Someone who will not judge you because he is in no position to judge."

Her gaze lingered on him for a moment. "You?"

"Me," he confirmed firmly. "Have you not heard about me?"

Her expression turned thoughtful. "I don't think so," she said. "But I remember hearing that Savernake had an Irish pirate for a relative."

"My father."

"I see," she said, her focus lingering on him as if appraising him. "Are you a pirate, too?"

He was. More than his father or brothers, Rory was a pirate and then some. His smuggling, however, was high-value merchandise – antiquities and rare jewels, mostly, things the *ton* adored but wouldn't let anyone know just how much they adored them. Even when these items were in their homes, they would make excuses… *Grandfather bought it on a trip…* or *this has been in my family for hundreds of years.* He'd smuggled ancient Greek frescos for an earl's dining room wall and artwork and stones from Baghdad for a duke's drawing room. The jewels he'd smuggled from Ceylon and Brazil were worn by the richest women in England.

Was he a pirate?

It was in his blood.

"I am many things," he said evasively, though it was the truth. "The point is that I have seen and done my share of questionable things. I do not judge people because I do not like to be judged, and if I promise not to repeat a word of our conversation, you can be assured that I will take it to my grave. Honestly, Miss Edith, you could not find a better Father Confessor. Now, what has this Forrester man done to you to upset you so?"

He was pointing to the bench that she'd been sitting on. Edie eyed the bench before lowering herself back onto it. But her gaze returned swiftly to Rory. She couldn't believe that she was actually considering answering his question, but there was a part of her that needed answers. She'd spent several years of her life pining for a man who had only lied to her and there was great confusion in that.

Great confusion in herself.

If she'd had any sense of self-worth, she would have kept her mouth shut.

But she didn't.

"I suppose he's done nothing that thousands of men haven't done before him," she said with a sigh. "Tell me something, Mr. Flynn – why do men lie to women so brazenly? Is it because they are fearful that the truth will not achieve the desired results? Or is it the mere fact that they feel powerful when manipulating a woman?"

Rory sat forward, elbows on his knees and his chin on his folded hands. "That is a question that has been asked for centuries," he said. "I do not think there is an easy answer."

"Have *you* lied to a woman?"

He snorted softly, averting his gaze. "I would be lying if I said I had not."

"Why did you do it?"

He shrugged, feeling the slightest bit uncomfortable. "Who knows?" he said. "Perhaps it seemed like a good idea at the time."

"Were you trying to control them?"

"Was Forrester trying to control you?"

She nodded, looking rather sickened. "He was," she said. Then she sighed heavily. "Of course, he was. He was a friend of my father's, you see. I say 'was' because their friendship has since ended because of me."

"How did he try to control you? What did he want you to do?"

"Become his mistress," she said, both ashamed and out-raged. "As if I am not worthy enough to be someone's wife. I have never been married, you see, and he wants me to be his mistress. If he cannot marry me, then he wants to keep me tucked away in the wilds of the north so that he may come to me at his convenience. That is all I will ever be to him – a convenience."

Rory was studying her. "But there is some feeling involved."

She hung her head. "I thought there was," she said. "To be perfectly honest, when I came to the Stag Ball, I thought I loved him. I thought I'd loved him since I'd met him, but now… it is so strange. Whatever I felt for him has vanished. His empty promises have drained it all away."

"That is because it was not real love," Rory said quietly.

"Are you certain?"

He nodded. "We have all had those moments with people we thought we loved but, in the end, what we thought was love vanished quite easily," he said. "You did not really love him, Miss Edith. You loved the idea of loving him and nothing more. It sounds as if he never did anything to earn your love."

She looked at him as if startled by the entire analysis. "That is the most appropriate thing I have ever heard," she said. "You are absolutely right – he never earned my love. He told me that I needed to prove *my* love for him, but he never did anything to prove his love for me. Not ever."

"Then you have your answer," Rory said.

It was true. She did. Edie looked at him as that realization settled but the truth was that she wasn't all that surprised.

Disappointed, but not surprised.

It took a stranger to help her figure that out.

"Good heavens," she muttered. "I suppose I always knew that. I suppose I wanted it to be true so badly that I tried to wish it so."

"There is no crime in that."

"I suppose," she said with some sadness. "I was young when I met him and simply believed what he told me."

"But now you are older and wiser."

"Older, anyway. I am not sure about wiser."

He smiled in the darkness. "But you have been counseled by me and that *will* make you wiser," he said. "Tell me, Miss Edith – what do you do when you are not in London, spending time at an unbearably formal ball?"

He was diverting the subject a little, which was a welcome relief. Edie could only talk about her failure so much.

"Ah, that is the great mystery," she said, smiling weakly. "What does a young woman do with all of her time when she has no home or husband to tend to?"

"Surely you must do great and creative things."

She laughed softly. "Perhaps only in my own mind," she said. "But surely you don't wish to speak about such things. You have an entire ball going on around you, yet you sit here with me in the orangery."

He shrugged. "I can think of worse things to do."

"Is this how you planned to spend your evening?"

It wasn't. He was reminded of Rose Halburton but, somehow, the lure of sad Edith Rhodes was greater than his lifelong sense of revenge at the moment. She was far and away more beautiful than Rose and perhaps that's why she had his attention, but there was something more to it. A little zing of excitement bolted through him whenever she laughed or smiled. That had his attention more than anything because it had never happened before.

It was quite intriguing.

"My evening was planned long before tonight," he said, which was true. It had been. "I would be honored with a dance if you are so inclined, however."

Edie's focus moved to the house beyond the orangery. "I am certain my mother is frantically searching for me," she said. "I'm sure word of the fight has spread through the ball by now and she is wondering where I am."

Rory nodded with some irony. "Nothing is more welcome than the fire of scandalous gossip," he said. "I can smell the smoke from here."

She grinned. "As can I," she said. "But I suspect I cannot stay here too much longer or else you and I might be caught up in a scandal of our own."

That was quite possibly true. Rory stood up and moved to the orangery doors, trying to get a look down the path at the garden. All he could see were people gathered around, undoubtedly watching the duke's men deal with the combatants.

Too many people made for too many witnesses.

He turned away.

"I would be happy to escort you inside while everyone's focus seems to be elsewhere," he said. "Shall we?"

Edie stood up. "Do you think we can leave now?"

He nodded. "I do," he said, reaching out to grasp her hand in a protective gesture. "Come with me."

She did.

Rory took Edie out of the orangery, through the darkened foliage, and into his grandfather's library. Because it was early in the evening, only a few men were gathered there and they were over by the hearth, undoubtedly partaking of the duke's fine tobacco that he had so generously provided for them. Rory and Edie slipped by, through the connecting door into the dining room, which was still being prepared at this point.

Rory came to a halt.

He stuck his head through the doorway leading into the main corridor to see who was about. The main entrance was off to his left, next to the library entrance, and the main staircase was in the entry. But a servants' staircase was directly in front of him, through a door, so he tugged on Edie's hand and they rushed across the hall and into the servants' corridor.

On the floor above were two massive drawing rooms with a door that connected them. The door, however, was collapsible and could be rolled back to make one giant ballroom. This was where the actual ball of the Stag Ball was taking place and once Rory took Edie up the stairs, she could simply slip into the ballroom as if she'd always been there. But before he let her go, Rory whispered to her.

"They are preparing to dance," he murmured, his eyes flicking over the crowd in the next room. "If you would like to dance with me, then you had better find your mother so that we may be properly introduced. It would not do for me to simply grab you and drag you to the dance floor."

She looked at him. "Who will introduce us?"

Rory gave her a rather sly look. "That is for me to know and you to find out," he said. "Go now, and find your mother. Do not stray from her. I will be along shortly. And try to be somewhere that I may easily find you."

"Where?"

"Near the windows."

It seemed as good a location as any, but Edie seemed hesitant. Rory could see that and he lifted his eyebrows at her. "You *do* wish to dance with me, don't you?"

Edie started to nod, but then she merely chuckled with some irony. "I did not think I would dance at all tonight," she said. "I thought I would be with… it does not matter now. What do you suppose has become of Myles?"

"Mr. Forrester?"

"Yes."

"I suspect he has either been escorted out or carried out, depending on how badly he was beaten." Rory watched her face for a moment before continuing. "Miss Edith, if you do not wish to dance at all, I would understand. Already, you have had a rather harrowing evening. Perhaps you simply wish to sit somewhere and rest."

She looked at him, studying his face, thinking that the man was incredibly handsome. But she couldn't think about him more than that. In fact, she wasn't entirely sure it was a good idea to dance with him because she'd only just discarded the only man she'd ever loved in a romantic sense or, perhaps more accurately, she'd only just freed herself.

But she knew she wasn't completely free. She and Myles had a history that couldn't be replaced. Somehow, she knew that Rory Flynn might make her forget all about Myles and then she'd be back where she started, only with another man. She simply didn't have the strength to fight off Rory's charm should he decide to overwhelm her with it.

"If I do, it will be alone," she said softly. "Mr. Flynn, you have been kind and chivalrous in a circumstance where you did not have to be. You could have just as easily left me to my own stupidity. But you did not and, for that, I am forever grateful. But I do believe it would be better if we were to part ways now."

He let go of her hand, which he had been holding the entire time. "I see," he said. "I've been quite clumsy, haven't I? I do apologize."

She shook her head. "Not at all," she said. "As I said, you've been kind and charming, but I think it would be best if we part friends."

"If I've not done something wrong, then why must we?"

"Because I don't think I want to be around any charming man right now and you, Mr. Flynn, have the capacity to disarm and enchant," she said, watching him grin. "You've given me so much to think about regarding Myles and I cannot thank you enough. But if I am to think clearly at all, it must be alone."

"For how long?"

"Beg pardon?"

"For how long?" he repeated, more firmly. "An hour? An evening? A day? How long?"

"I don't know," she said. "Does it matter?"

He scratched his ear, a nervous gesture. "Perhaps not," he said. "But if I want to call upon you to see how you are faring, how long must I wait?"

Her brow furrowed. "Why on earth would you want to call upon me again?"

"I told you. To see how you are."

"I am fine."

"Clearly not if you must go off and become a hermit, away from all men."

She started to giggle. "It will not be forever."

"Good," he said. "Will you be able to entertain male friends by tomorrow? You see, there is always a garden party after the Stag Ball at my father's estate in London near Teddington. I should like to invite you and your family to attend."

"Your *father's* home?"

He nodded. "My father does not attend the Stag Ball, but he allows my grandfather to use the property for his garden party," he said. "My grandfather only invites close friends and their families. I would like to invite you."

She didn't give him any indication that she would accept the invitation. "Why does your father not attend the ball?" she asked. "And where is your mother? Is she here?"

Rory shook his head. "She does not attend, either."

"Why not?"

He peered at her strangely. "Miss Edith, if you know of my family and have heard the rumors, you need not pretend to be ignorant of it all," he said. "I thought we were more honest with each other than that."

She genuinely had no idea what he meant. "I know nothing of your family," she said. "Should I?"

His eyebrows lifted. "You mean that you are the only person in London who does not know of the Sinning Flynns?"

She looked at him with surprise. "The Sinning Flynns?" she said. Then she chuckled. "Is *that* who you are?"

"Ah," he said with something that sounded like satisfaction. "You see? You have heard of us."

"I think so," she said. "We live a life at Everton in South Yorkshire that is far removed from London, so my trips here are not terribly frequent. I've heard of the Sinning Flynns, but I do not recall if I was told they are related to Savernake."

"We are," he said. "My father was an Irish pirate who was granted an earldom from a grateful king. My father kept many a supply line open in the West Indies and the English Channel and he was amply rewarded by King George. He became the Earl of Sinbrook and married my mother, who was betrothed to another man. Our sinning days started before I was even born."

Edie was listening with a surprising amount of interest. "I suspect there is a good deal more to your story," she said. "Much more than you can tell me in one night."

Rory grinned. "I can tell you tomorrow at the garden party."

"You will have to speak with my mother."

"Go and find her. I will be along shortly."

With that, the conversation seemed to come to an end, but it wasn't awkward. In truth, there was some anticipation in the air, at least as far as Rory was concerned. He hadn't felt like that in a very long time, as misplaced and unexpected as it was. Edie was easy to talk to and they seemed to have an excellent rapport, which was quite unusual for him. He wasn't easy to talk to, nor did he ever have a good rapport, with anyone. He wasn't quite sure what made Edie special, but something did.

Something, indeed.

CHAPTER EIGHT

"WHAT DID HE say his name was?"

Edie had never seen her mother look quite so shocked. Near the windows of the grand ballroom, on the side of the house that overlooked the infamous garden, she had just told her mother a lie. Well, not all of it was a lie. She had just told her mother that although she had failed to find her friends, she'd met a very polite young man who had helped her when she'd become lost. The only part that was truthful was the part about meeting a polite young man.

It was the man's name that had her mother up in arms.

"Rory Flynn," Edie repeated patiently. "He is the grandson of the Duke of Savernake. You wanted me to meet a young man and I have, Mother. He's utterly wonderful."

Henrietta stared at her daughter. "Rory Flynn," she said. "Good heavens, Child... a Flynn?"

"He's the duke's grandson," Edie said with a hint of sarcasm. "The man is going to be at his grandfather's event. Why is that so shocking?"

Henrietta took a deep breath. "It is not shocking in and of itself," she said. Then, she rolled her eyes in frustration. "When I brought you here to meet a young man, that directive did not include a Sinning Flynn."

"Why does everyone call them the Sinning Flynns?" Edie asked, sounding as if the entire thing were ridiculous. "I've heard that name mentioned, but why do people say that?"

Henrietta looked around to make sure they weren't being heard. She spied Matilda in a group of other young people, laughing and chatting, before continuing. Thank God they weren't present to hear what she had to say.

"Because they are nothing but Irish scum," she muttered. "Sean Flynn stole Savernake's daughter away from Lord Exford many years ago and married her. She had four children, all boys, and all just as dark and reckless as their father. They are notorious, Edie, and Rory most of all. The man is a legend in London and Cornwall and he's not even seen his thirtieth year."

Edie was listening with great interest. "Notorious?" she repeated, aghast. "How would you know that?"

Henrietta's eyes narrowed. "Don't be stupid," she hissed. "I have been around the *ton* enough to know the gossip. And… and years ago, I knew Amy Wellesbourne. She was such a sweet girl and so very pretty. If you must know, she was far too good for John Halburton, but he was a smart match. She would have had everything had she married him. Instead, she fell for that… that *pirate.*"

Edie didn't much care about Sean Flynn or even Amy Wellesbourne. But she did care about Rory Flynn.

"But what about Rory?" she said. "You said he is a legend in

London. I've never even heard of him."

"Good," Henrietta said firmly. "But so you know why you must stay away from him, I will tell you – they say that Rory Flynn is a smuggler and not just any smuggler. No! The man smuggles rare antiquities and jewels for those who can pay him. He also owns gambling dens in London, one he won from the owner, and those who know about it say the place is called Gomorrah. A man can bet on anything at all at Gomorrah."

Edie was enthralled. She wasn't going to deny it. "Gomorrah?" she said. "Like the wicked city in the bible?"

"That is why they call the place Gomorrah!"

Edie had to fight off a smile. She thought it all sounded incredibly scandalous and, truthfully, incredibly exciting, but if her mother knew she was thinking such things, the woman would lock her up in a closet and throw away the key. Therefore, she kept her enthusiasm to herself.

For the moment.

"He seemed quite nice to me," she said. "He didn't seem wicked at all."

"That is how they seduce you," Henrietta said. "Silken tongues breed silken words until a woman is hypnotized by them. Don't be hypnotized, Edie. The man is trouble and he is far and away an unsuitable match. I did not spend the last two years hiding you from Polite Society for you to ruin your life again and possibly Tilly's as well. If Myles Forrester was bad, Rory Flynn is worse. You don't seem to have the best judgment when it comes to men, Edie."

Edie wasn't happy to hear those words. They were insulting even if they were true. But she'd hoped her mother would have been impressed by her informal acquaintance with Rory Flynn, but that wasn't to be. If anything, she was downright averse to the entire suggestion that a duke's grandson should be a suitable prospect.

"Who *is* suitable, Mother?" she asked, her gaze moving over the ballroom with its finely dressed women and dashing men. "You've been quite free to tell me who is not suitable, but who is? Keeping in mind that I am damaged goods, who is to your taste, Mother?"

Henrietta looked at her sharply. "You'll not take that tone with me," she said in a low voice. "Do as I say, Edie, and you shall have a happy and fulfilling life. Follow your childish and irresponsible instincts and you shall only know ruin. Which choice will it be?"

Edie was growing weary of her mother's constant demands. She was so rigid that it made Edie feel as if she were choking somehow, unable to breathe, unable to simply live her life the way she wanted to live it… and with whom.

It wasn't fair.

She felt as if she should have a say in her own happiness.

"He's a duke's grandson," she finally said. "And from what you've said, he's wildly rich. What more could you ask for in a husband for your eldest daughter?"

Henrietta sighed heavily. "I will not discuss this with you."

"He has invited us to the garden party the duke is giving tomorrow," she said, glancing around the ballroom in the hope of locating the elusive Flynn son. "His father has a townhome near Teddington and we have all been invited."

Henrietta looked at her as if she'd just announced her decision to murder the pope. "He *what*?" she hissed. "He invited you – *us* – to Sean Flynn's home?"

By the time Edie looked at her mother, the woman was fanning herself furiously because she'd grown lightheaded at the mere suggestion of attending an event at the home of the notorious pirate. Forcing herself to show some concern, Edie reached out to grasp her mother's arm.

"Let us find you a chair so you do not fall down and embarrass us all," she said. "Breathe, Mother. You needn't be so dramatic."

Henrietta wouldn't move in spite of her daughter trying to force her towards the nearest chair. "If it is ever known that one of the Sinning Flynns has invited us to a social event, it will be our ruin," she said. "You must never tell anyone that, Edie. Not even your silly friends."

Edie couldn't help but feel disappointment. "Then we will not go?"

"Most assuredly not," Henrietta said with more force than she should have. "In fact, I… good heavens. What is *he* doing here?"

She was looking off into the ballroom. Edie had no idea what her mother meant until she turned to see what had the woman so shocked. Coming in through one of the doors to the ballroom was none other than Myles himself, holding a handkerchief up to a swelling lip.

Normally, she would have been thrilled to see him and already plotting to have a dance or two with the man. Or slipping away with him. That kind of behavior had been infused into her heart and soul since she'd met the man. But as she looked at him, all she could manage to feel was enormous disappointment. The conversation in the garden rolled around in her head, emphasizing just how foolish she'd been.

She was finished making the biggest mistake of her young life.

Quickly, she turned away.

"Let us go into another room," she said. "Surely there are refreshments, somewhere."

In her grip, Henrietta seemed to come to life. All around them were the sights and smells of an opulent ball – the smell of the candles as they burned heavily in the stale air, the smell of perfume and powder, even the smell of the walls that had been freshly painted for the occasion. Lights were blazing, jewels were glistening, and women were trying their best to show off their expensive and custom gowns.

But Henrietta didn't seem to notice any of that at the moment.

She grabbed Edie by the hand.

"Come," she hissed, moving swiftly through the crowd as she dragged her daughter. When she came to Matilda in a group of young adults, she nearly broke Matilda's wrist when she grabbed her. "Come, Tilly. Come now, quickly."

Matilda was yanked away, back through the ballroom, down the stairs, and out the front of the townhome.

Across the road in the square, the bonfire was still in the process of being prepared. Henrietta approached one of the footmen and demanded their carriage be brought around. As the footman went running, Edie finally managed to break her mother's grip.

"What on earth are you doing?" she said. "Why did you order the carriage?"

Henrietta was rattled. She focused on her eldest daughter with a wild look in her eyes.

"Because we are leaving," she said, almost in tears. "First, you make an acquaintance with one of the Flynn brothers, enough so that he invites you to a garden party on the morrow. Then, Myles Forrester coincidentally makes an appearance. I am not stupid, Edith. Not a decent man in sight, but you are gathering rogues and rakes of the worst kind and I will not stand for it. I do not know what it is about you, but you attract the undesirables. I'll not have it tonight and I'll not have you ruining Tilly's reputation before she even has a chance to earn one. Even if you are a lost cause, she is not. We are *leaving*!"

Matilda, realizing that they were departing, broke down in tears. Her accusing eyes turned to Edie, who was greatly ashamed by her mother's accusations. She couldn't even look her sister in the eyes.

Mostly because Henrietta was right.

She did attract the worst kind.

Edie stood off to the side until the carriage was brought around, hurt and ashamed. Perhaps leaving was best. She didn't want to see Myles and even if Rory Flynn had a horrible reputation, she still wasn't worthy of him. Her mother had made that clear. Duke's grandson or not, smuggler or saint, she wasn't worthy of any of them.

It was time to go home.

For Edie Rhodes, the Stag Ball had come to an end.

CHAPTER NINE

"Ambition is never wasted on a ruthless man."
Sin Commandment #9

H E NEVER SAW her again.

Rory spent the rest of the evening looking for Edie and the more he looked, the more confused he became. Women just didn't vanish into thin air, but Edie had apparently done just that.

She'd gone off to find her mother and that was the last time he saw her, so there was some concern with that. He searched the entire bottom floor of the townhome looking for her and when he reached the ballroom, dancing had already commenced. He caught sight of his brother and had a few words with him because in his search for Edie, he'd heard something about a lady his brother had been seen dancing with. A lady whose family reputation seemed to be tarnished. After teasing his brother about it, which Aidan wasn't so keen on, he continued on in his quest.

But there was no sign of her.

He might have thought her abducted by the man he saw her

with earlier in the evening, but Forrester was dancing. He saw him, bloodied lip and all, dancing with a young woman who seemed quite enamored with him. He wondered why the duke's men had allowed him to stay, but he couldn't give it much thought beyond that.

He was on the hunt.

Rose Halburton caught his attention as he passed from one side of the ballroom to the other. She was standing with her sister and father, watching the dancing, perhaps hoping that someone would ask her to dance. Rory knew it should be him; that's what he'd planned. For years and years, he'd planned this moment with Exford's daughter, and now that the timing was perfect, he simply couldn't bring himself to do it.

What in the hell is the matter with me?

Everything had fallen into place. Exford's daughter was available, with no male attention, and it would have been so easy for him to slide in and charm her. Perhaps have a dance or two before stealing her away from her father, out into the orangery, where he would proceed to seduce her. While the earl would be frantically looking for her, he would be compromising her. *That was the plan, damn it all!* A kiss, a touch, and she would be his but he had to make that move. Years of humiliation to his mother and those degrading years at Oxford demanded it.

Yet… he was distracted.

Edie.

As he watched, one of the duke's men walked up to Exford and introduced a tall, pale, and homely young man to Rose. She smiled. A dance was offered.

And Rory didn't particularly care.

Was it possible his sense of vengeance could be so easily

forgotten?

Evidently so because he turned away from the ballroom and continued his search for Edie. He'd known the woman all of an hour and, already, he was attracted to her as he'd never been attracted to a woman in his life. She was exquisite and she smelled of blossoms, but there were other women who were exquisite and smelled of flowers. He simply couldn't figure out what made Edie so different.

Perhaps there was a kindred spirit there.

That brought him pause.

He remembered what Forbes had told him, how rumors suggested that Edie had been seen in a tavern's stable with an older man, and Rory would have thought that only to be vicious gossip except for the fact that he saw her in the arms of the man who evidently *was* her love. Or at least, had been. A married man who had promised to leave his wife for her but who had lied about it.

Edie had known scandal and betrayal.

She wasn't alone in that shame.

That's where Rory felt that she was a kindred spirit. So many women at the ball this evening had impeccable reputations, something their families worked hard for. Rory wasn't worthy of any of them and he truly didn't care. But Edie…

She was different.

If what he'd heard was true, then he'd found a woman who was as flawed as he was.

Rory ended up outside in the front of the townhome, with the bonfire being set up in the square across the street and the night above still and cold. He asked one of the footmen if he'd seen a pretty woman in a lavender gown and the footman answered that he had. He told Rory that the lady had left not an hour before but he could tell him no more than that.

It was time to find his grandfather.

After meeting Edie, he'd planned to have his grandfather introduce him to her formally since he wanted to dance with her, but now that she was gone, he wanted to pick the old duke's brain. Savernake knew everyone who was anyone and surely the man would know who Viscount Rossington was. He wanted to find out where the man lived.

Where Rossington was, Edie more than likely would be.

Unfortunately, it was hours before he was able to speak with his grandfather. For such a frail, old man, he'd held up admirably for the ball. It wasn't until after the midnight buffet had been spread out that Rory was able to speak with the man as he wearily retired to his bedroom.

When he did, Rory was waiting for him.

"Why aren't you feasting with the rest of them?" the duke asked as he shuffled into his room.

Rory had been sitting in a chair in the duke's big chamber, half-asleep at the late hour.

"Because I wanted to speak with you," he said. "This might be my only opportunity."

The duke's valet had been following him but when the old man heard Rory's statement, he paused and looked at his grandson with some trepidation. In spite of the fact that he'd all but told Rory bluntly that he supported any act of vengeance against Exford, he was still leery to hear about it. He shooed his valet out of the room and had the man close the door. Only then did he dare to speak.

"Very well," he said. "You may speak. What have you done?"

Rory scratched his head. "Nothing," he said. "If you are

referring to Exford, I did… nothing."

"Why not?"

Rory shrugged. "Tonight was not the night," he said, somewhat lying about it because he was feeling such confusion. "Too many people, I suppose. And perhaps… perhaps it's best not to shame the man in your home. That would reflect badly upon you and the more I think about it, the more I don't want to do that to you. Let my vengeance on Exford happen somewhere else, away from you. I'd not thought much of you and how my actions affect you and, for that, I apologize. I'm a selfish man, Doody."

The duke looked at him in surprise at the mention of a very old nickname, the very name Rory would use to taunt Aidan with. Then, he started to chuckle.

"Do my ears deceive me?" he said. "Is it possible that Rory the Rogue is actually growing up? Maturing? Because that is something a mature man would say, my boy."

Rory was uncomfortable with the suggestion that he had changed. "Rory the Rogue is alive and well," he said. "I may go down, but I do not want to drag you with me. Yet, have no doubt that I will exact vengeance against Exford. But not here. It is not the right place nor the right time."

The duke nodded his head as if accepting that. "If that is the way you feel," he said. "You've waited a very long time only to back away from your victory."

"I've not backed away. I've simply decided tonight was not the night."

"Is that what you've come to tell me?"

Rory nodded. "That," he said. "And I want to ask you something."

"What is it?"

"Do you know Viscount Rossington?"

The duke sighed wearily as he made his way over to the bed. "Frederick Rhodes," he said. "I know him. Why?"

"Where does he live?"

The duke sat down heavily. "Over in Belgravia," he said. "As I recall, it's called Rossington House. The largest home on Belgravia Square, if I recall correctly."

"*What* do you know about him?" Rory asked carefully. "About his family?"

The duke yawned. "They have property near Doncaster, as I recall," he said. "The viscount's family is rich in cattle. They're quite wealthy."

"And he has children?"

"Daughters, I believe," the duke said. Then he eyed his grandson strangely. "Why so many questions? What's on your mind?"

Rory shrugged. "I met the eldest daughter this evening," he said. "Quite by accident, really, but I was going to have you properly introduce us when she suddenly disappeared."

"What do you mean?"

"Precisely that," Rory said. "She went to find her mother and I never saw her again after that. The footmen told me that she had left with her family. Before the dancing even started, they went home."

The duke shrugged. "Perhaps she fell ill," he said. "Why is it of such import to you?"

Rory didn't want to tell him why. If he did, the duke might figure out why he hadn't gone after Exford's daughter.

He'd been distracted by another woman.

God, that made him sound so shallow.

"Because I saved her from a rather unsavory situation and I

feel some responsibility for her," he finally ventured. "Perhaps I should go to Belgravia tonight to make sure she is well."

The duke put up a hand. "Rory, if you want to go to Belgravia to pluck the viscount's daughter from her bed, that is your business," he said. "But do not lie about it. I still do not know what you've come to tell me other than you decided not to take your revenge on Exford tonight and there's a viscount's daughter you wish to ravage."

Rory shook his head. "It's not like that," he said. "I do not wish to ravage her."

"Then what?"

Rory was closer to a personal confession than he'd ever been in his life, but his interaction with the duke this night had made him feel closer to the man than he ever had. It would be so easy to confess everything to a man he'd always adored.

Still...

"I always wished I'd had the relationship with you that Aidan has," he muttered in an unguarded moment. "Growing up, I always envied Aidan. He is your favorite."

The duke gazed at him in the dim chamber light. "He is the only one out of all of your brothers, including you, who took the time to form a relationship with me," he said, his tone softer. "Carmack and Kellen were always off forging their own way and you... you simply didn't need me. You didn't need anyone."

"I don't think that's true," Rory said quietly. "I didn't think anyone cared, so I pretended that I did not need anyone. A self-fulfilling prophesy, I'm afraid."

The duke nodded his head slowly. "You were the stubborn one," he said. "A sullen and determined child."

"And lonely."

The duke stared at him a moment before smiling. "That is the first time I've ever heard you give a hint of human emotion," he said. "I am seeing more of that mature man."

Rory smirked. "Then here is much more from that mature man," he said. "I have asked you about Rossington's daughter because I am attracted to her. Not in the usual way. I have no desire to sneak into her bedchamber while her parents sleep in the next room. She… she's different somehow. She left just as I was coming to know her."

The duke sensed something quite different from his grandson and that caused him to stand up and move in Rory's direction.

"Is she the reason you failed to move forward with your plans for Exford?" he asked.

Rory couldn't look him in the eyes but, after a moment, he sighed heavily and hung his head. "There is no use lying," he said. "I don't know what happened. All I know is that I met a woman who made me feel as I've never felt in my life and just when I was coming to know her, she left. I had a perfect opportunity with Rose Halburton and I did not take it because I was too preoccupied with Edie."

"Edie?"

"Rossington's daughter."

The old duke looked down upon Amy's third-born son. In today's society, the third-born sons were usually meant for the clergy, but that had never been an option for Rory. He'd been born with fire in him and, until today, the duke wondered if that was all Rory would ever be – full of fire and recklessness. But at this moment, he saw something from Rory he never thought he would.

Feeling.

"You came to me today as a boy," he said, putting a hand on Rory's shoulder. "But for the first time in my eyes, you have actually become a man. I cannot tell you how pleased I am, Rory. I am glad I lived to see it."

Rory was torn between embarrassment and warmth. His grandfather had never said such things to him before so it was difficult to know how to react.

"I suppose we must all grow up sometime, although I'm not exactly sure I've changed all that much," he said. "We were only speaking of a woman, after all."

"A special woman, evidently," the duke said. Then he dropped his hand from Rory's shoulder and went to the table against the wall, the one he'd had imported all the way from Italy with its leather-bound top and legs of gold leaf. There was a crystal decanter on top of the table, filled with dark red liquid, and he poured a measure into a small, crystal glass. "Rory, there is something you should know."

"What is it?"

The duke looked at him. "I'm dying," he said quietly. "I have a cancer that is slowly killing me. It has been going on for some time, but now I am at the end. My physician feels that in a week or two, I will be bed bound. Death will not be far behind. I wasn't going to tell you, but given our exchange tonight, I am comfortable to confide such things in you."

Rory was trying to keep the expression of horror off his face. "But… but that's not possible," he said. Even as he said it, he was looking at a man who was far from the robust grandfather he had known all his life. His grandfather had even alluded to his health earlier in the evening, so his confession shouldn't have come as a surprise. "Surely it cannot be. Surely there is…"

The duke put up a hand to silence him. "Denial will not

make it so," he said. "The diagnosis has been confirmed. But I want to tell you personally a few things, now that we have this time together. As you know, your Uncle Martin will inherit the title and properties, although I do have an unentailed property that I have offered to Aidan."

Rory's eyebrows lifted. "Aidan?"

"If he marries before I die."

Rory's mouth popped open in surprise. "And he agreed?"

The duke fought off a grin. "I am not certain if he actually agreed," he said. "But let us not speak of Aidan right now. I want to speak of you. Are you serious about this Rhodes woman?"

Rory still wasn't over the fact that not only was his grandfather dying, the man was offering property to his youngest brother. "I don't know," he said. "All I know is that one conversation has made me feel as I've never felt in my life. One simple conversation with a woman who knew my family name and she didn't run away. It was *one* conversation, Grandfather, but a conversation that I could have quite happily engaged in forever."

The duke sipped the brandy in the little glass before speaking. "When I met your grandmother, she made me feel like that," he said. "How odd that you and I should have such similarities, Rory. It seems to me that you may be serious about her, indeed."

"Possibly."

"What of Exford's daughter?"

Rory sighed. "Somehow, it seems oddly unimportant," he said. "It makes no sense because I have been planning this for years. How can I forget about something so important?"

"Simple," the duke said. "It involves another woman. You

cannot think of another woman when your focus, and possibly your heart, lies elsewhere. Vengeance pales by comparison to love."

Rory eyed him. "I *don't* love her."

"Not now," the duke said. "But she has your attention enough that she has made you forget your vengeance. Do not diminish the significance of that."

"Aye," Rory sighed softly. "She has my attention."

"Do you want my advice? You have never wanted it before."

"I may not now, but what is it?"

The duke laughed softly. That reply sounded much more like the Rory he knew. "If she makes you feel like the sun is rising on a new day, then find her," he said. "If she makes you feel as if you cannot breathe or you cannot remember your own name when you look into her eyes, then find her. Even if you don't know how, exactly, you feel about her, find out. Life is too short not to take an opportunity when it comes. I wish I had more time for more opportunities. For me, Rory... take this opportunity."

Rory looked at him seriously. "But what if her father will not receive me?" he asked, genuinely fearful. "That has never mattered to me until this very moment. What do I do?"

The duke set his glass down and turned to him. "I have two weeks or less before this poison inside of me weakens me too much," he said. "Find your lady. If she is all you imagine her to be, you will tell me and I will send word to her father. I cannot offer you lands or properties. I cannot even offer you money. There is nothing I have that you do not already have more of. But I can offer you my support. Let me do this for you, Rory. If it is what you truly want."

Rory stood up, feeling closer to his grandfather than he ever had. It was joy he'd never known. "It is," he said. "I am sure it is. And I am sorry that we were never closer, Grandfather."

"We are now. Go and find her."

Rory didn't have to be told twice.

CHAPTER TEN

"Women are always, invariably, hiding something."
Sin Commandment #10

"Mama says we are leaving for home tomorrow," Matilda said sadly. "Why, Edie? Why are we leaving?"

Edie knew why but it would not have made sense to Matilda if she told her the truth. She'd had all night to think about it and she'd come to the conclusion that perhaps her mother was right. Matilda was young and untouched by scandal and all Edie seemed to be doing was trying to ruin her sister's chances by bleeding her questionable reputation onto her. Guilt by association, as it were.

Edie simply couldn't give her a straight answer.

"Perhaps she misses home," she finally said. "We did enjoy the Stag Ball for the short time we were there, didn't we?"

Matilda nodded, though she was becoming tearful. "I don't want to leave," she said. "We have been planning for this all year. I don't understand why we must leave."

They were sitting in the mews alleyway of Rossington House, back behind the house where the conveyances and horses were kept. There was peace here, away from their parents. Around them, the usual collection of dogs and cats roamed about and that included Matilda's little dog. Edie put her arm around Matilda's shoulders to comfort the confused and sad young woman, while keeping an eye on the brown and white dog.

"Did you ask Mama why?" Edie asked quietly.

Matilda nodded, sniffling. "She told me that it was none of my affair," she said. "Did I do something wrong, Edie?"

Edie shook her head. "No," she sighed. "I did."

"What did you do?"

"I spoke to the wrong man."

"What man?"

Edie wasn't sure what, or how, to tell her. Matilda was growing up, that was true, but she didn't know about her older sister's escapes with Myles Forrester. Edie was still pure and virtuous in Matilda's eyes and Edie wanted to keep it that way.

"A man with a bad reputation," she said. "I didn't know it at the time, however, so I will tell you that he was very kind to me. Kinder than… well, it does not matter, but suffice it to say that he was extremely kind and he invited us to a garden party, but when I told Mama, she thought the man's reputation was a questionable one and we could not accept. And that is why we left the ball last night. Mama was afraid that the man would lure us into his seedy world with his invitation. She did it to protect us."

Matilda actually understood that explanation and it didn't put Edie too much in a bad light. "Oh," Matilda said, her tears fading. "Why didn't she tell us?"

Edie gave her a squeeze. "Because you were upset enough," she said. "Mama was upset, too. Did you not notice? She didn't want you to beg her to remain because it was a difficult decision for her to make. No one runs from the Stag Ball."

Matilda thought on the situation with surprising clarity for a girl on the cusp of womanhood. "The man," she said. "What was his name?"

"The one who invited us to the garden party?"

"Yes."

"Rory Flynn," Edie said, thinking on the man with the dark hair and flashing eyes. "The Honorable Rory Flynn. His father is the Earl of Sinbrook."

"An earl's son?" Matilda said with some excitement in her voice. "Why would Mama not want us to attend his party?"

"Because the Earl of Sinbrook is Irish," Edie said. "He is not of the best reputation, nor is his son, though I did not realize the extent of it. He seemed so… perfect."

Matilda was watching her face. "You like him."

It wasn't a question. Edie didn't have to think very much about it. "I do," she said. "He didn't speak to me like Mama and Papa do, as if I were a wayward child, or even like Myles, who speaks to me as if I only have half a brain in my head. He spoke to me as if I were a responsible and respectable woman. As if my thoughts and actions mattered."

Matilda, though she was young, could still understand that it had meant something to her sister. But she also recognized a name that was taboo in her house – *Myles.*

"You still speak of Myles?" she said. "Mama shushes you when you do."

Edie sighed faintly and looked away, back to the dog that was now finding a place in the sun to lie down. "I will speak of him no more," she said. "Remember something, Tilly – remember that men will often say things to trick a woman into doing something she does not want to do. You've not had experience with men yet, but when you do… be cautious. They only mean to bring you to ruin."

"Not always."

It wasn't Matilda who replied. Startled, Edie turned to see the very reason for fleeing the Stag Ball the night before.

Rory Flynn in the flesh.

❧

"YOU'RE SURE SHE'LL be here?" Forbes asked. "Then why have I come? I have no desire to see the woman."

Rory grinned. Seated next to Forbes in his fashionable barouche, the one he called *Darling Libby* because, in his words, "like a woman, a coach needs to be handled". He watched the scenery go by as they headed south towards Belgravia.

"But I do," he said. "You're here in case I need a decoy. I was thinking about it all morning, Forbes. I know why she left the Stag Ball."

"Why?"

"Because I chased her out," Rory said with some disgust. "Think about it – I saved her from disgrace only to invite her to dance with me which, for a woman of her stature, would be as bad as if I had molested her in public. I'm not a man women want to be seen with. At least, not respectable women."

Forbes yawned. He'd gone to bed at dawn, like everyone else who had attended the Stag Ball, only to have Rory pounding on his door a few hours later and demanding he bring around his barouche because they had a journey to make to Belgravia. It bumped down the avenue, avoiding pedestrians who were going about their business on this breezy day.

"You have enough women that want to be seen with you

that you should never be lonely a day in your life," Forbes said. "What makes this one so special?"

"Because she is."

He sounded final, as if he didn't want further questions about her. Forbes knew that tone well.

"As you say," he grumbled. "But why am I to be a decoy?"

"In case I need you to call upon the family and distract them so I can prowl around looking for Miss Edith," Rory said. "If she's there, I will find her."

Forbes simply shook his head. "It all seems like a great deal of trouble for just one woman."

"I told you. She's not just any woman."

"I'm coming to suspect that."

They entered the area of Belgravia Square, with the verdant lawns attracting an array of people on this fine day. While Forbes was watching the women, Rory was watching the townhomes. *The largest home on the square*, his grandfather had told him. They made their way around the square, avoiding people and other conveyances, until Rory spied what he thought was, indeed, the largest home on the square.

All of the homes were built from sand-colored stone, four stories tall and sometimes five. The architecture was strong, with pillars guarding doorways and thick, solid walls. Rory had Forbes pull his barouche to a halt just past the largest home on the square and he climbed out onto the sidewalk.

"Well?" Forbes said. "Where are you going?"

Rory was looking at the enormous structure that had his attention. "There," he said, pointing. "Grandfather said it was the largest home on the square and that looks like the largest to me. Doesn't it?"

Forbes craned his neck back to study it. "It's big," he agreed.

"Why would a mere viscount have such a large place?"

Rory shrugged. "Grandfather says the family is obscenely wealthy," he said. "Cattle, evidently."

Forbes yawned again. "Now that we're here, what do you want me to do?"

Rory's gaze glittered with the prospect of seeing Edie. "I am not certain," he said. "Drive around the square a few times and if I don't come running out and jump in for a fast departure, park somewhere within sight of this place and I will find you. Whatever you do, don't leave."

Forbes wasn't so sure this was a good idea, but he didn't argue. "I won't," he said. "But when you're finished with this, I want to return to The Lyon's Den. I lost a small fortune there over the past couple of days that I need to reclaim."

Rory held up a hand, essentially agreeing with him, but his focus was on the house. As Forbes pulled away, mingling with some traffic, Rory headed towards the townhome that had a big balcony on the second floor, projecting over the walkway like a masthead. But as he approached, he began to think of a plan. Now that he was here, what was he going to do? It wasn't as if he could walk up to the door and announce himself.

That brought him to a stop.

No, he couldn't go to the front door. But perhaps he could go to the back door. Perhaps there was a servant back in the mews that he could pay for information.

Perhaps that was the place to start.

Turning in the opposite direction, he walked quickly down the street and rounded the corner. There was less foot traffic on the side street as he hunted for the mews, which he found quickly. There was a massive arch over the entry to the long, narrow alleyway and he headed into the area where horses and carriages were stored for the entire block.

There were both men and women working back here, tending horses or cleaning carriages. It was a busy world, with dogs barking and cats darting across his path. As he neared the house he'd targeted for Rossington House, he noticed a dog running about and a few cats.

And then, he saw her.

He couldn't believe the luck.

Even at a distance, he could see Edie with her sister, sitting on a wooden bench. A smile crossed his lips at the sight of her, realizing he'd been right all along. This *was* Rossington House and he'd been fortunate enough to locate the exact person he wished to see. No paying servants, no sneaking around.

He'd found her.

Moving closer to the mews themselves, he came up on Edie's left side. She'd been talking to her sister, focused on their conversation, and hadn't noticed him. As he came to within a few feet of her, he heard her say something about men driving women to ruin.

He couldn't help his answer.

"Not always," he said quietly.

The young woman next to Edie was startled by his answer and gasped as she turned to him. Edie was a little slower to react, but not by much. When their eyes met, she bolted up from the bench, her eyes wide at him.

"Mr. Flynn," she gasped. "How… what are you doing here?"

He smiled. The woman had been beautiful in the moonlight, but it hadn't done her justice. In the daylight, she was positively radiant.

"I was traveling through Belgravia and thought I might take a chance that you would be in residence," he said. "You left the ball last night before we were properly introduced and I feared for your health and safety. Are you well, Miss Edith?"

Edie nodded, still in disbelief that Rory was standing in front of her. "I'm quite well," she said. She could feel her sister pressing against her and she indicated the young woman. "This is my sister, Matilda."

Rory acknowledged the pale, younger woman. "I see that beauty runs in the family," he said, smiling. "It is an honor, Miss Matilda. Did you enjoy the ball last night?"

Matilda flushed furiously. "We left early," she said. "But… but I liked it while I was there."

"Good," he said. "I am sure there will be many more that you will be invited to."

"I hope so."

The silence that followed was slightly awkward. Rory wanted to speak to Edie, but her sister seemed permanently attached to her hip. He wasn't sure how to ask the girl to leave, so he cleared his throat softly and went to the point.

"May I have a word with you, Miss Edith?" he asked. "Without an audience, preferably."

Edie had no idea what he meant until she saw him look at Matilda. Being that she was thrilled to see him, and didn't mind a private word with him, she turned to her sister.

But there could be… complications.

Her heart began to race.

"Tilly, I want you to keep an eye out for Mama," she instructed quietly. "Go to the garden gate and watch for her. If you see her coming, you will tell me quickly. Please?"

"But do not go too far," Rory said, a twinkle in his eyes. "Your sister must be chaperoned when speaking to an unmarried man."

Matilda's eyes widened. "Me?" she said. "I'm the chaperone?"

Rory nodded, grinning, and Matilda's gaze lingered on him for a moment before she sauntered over to the gate that led towards the garden of Rossington House and, subsequently, the house itself. When she was far enough away but still close enough to bear witness, Edie turned to Rory.

"How on earth did you find me?" she asked, incredulous.

Rory's grin was back. "I asked my grandfather what he knew of your father and he told me about Rossington House," he said. "I assumed you would be here, so I took a chance. I wanted to know why you left before the ball ended last night. Was it something I did?"

Edie wasn't sure how to reply. Was it something he did? Of course it was, but it was a lifelong string of actions and not simply one. She wasn't sure how she could tell him without insulting him.

"My... my mother wasn't feeling well so we had no choice but to leave," she said. "I am sorry I wasn't able to bid you a farewell and thank you for what you did for me."

He waved her off. "It was nothing, but you are welcome," he said. "I wanted to tell you that I very much enjoyed speaking to you and I was wondering... wondering if I could speak with you again sometime. I should like to call on you, Miss Edith. My grandfather is more than happy to make the proper introduction to your parents."

Edie was more than thrilled to hear his intentions. Under normal circumstances, she would have been positively giddy, but it simply wouldn't do. After what her mother had said about him and his family last night, she was quite certain her mother would not receive Rory Flynn. Perhaps it was best that he know it at the start, as disappointing as it was for her to tell him.

She couldn't let the man make a fool of himself.

"I am not certain that is possible," she said with regret. "Mr. Flynn, I…"

"Rory. Please call me Rory."

She eyed him a moment. Calling the man by his first name was quite forward but, then again, the entire association with him had been unconventional.

"Very well," she said hesitantly. "Rory, I'm not certain that would be possible. You see… oh, blast it all. You may as well know the truth. My mother wasn't ill last night. I told her you had invited us to a garden party and she proceeded to tell me that I was to have nothing to do with you. That was why we left. For that reason and also for the fact that she saw Myles in the ballroom. She panicked. She thinks that I am going down the merry path to ruin. Perhaps she's right."

Rory wasn't surprised to hear that. He'd known it all along. But he was disappointed. "I see," he said. "Thank you for being honest. What did she say about me?"

Edie sighed heavily and averted her gaze. "That you were a smuggler, like your father."

"I am."

"I asked you and you did not give me a direct answer."

"I told you that I was many things – and I am. Importing goods is one of my business ventures."

She cocked her head, studying him intently as the breeze blew her dark hair across her face. Perhaps there was a hint of surrender in her expression.

Truth had a way of breaking down those barriers.

"I want you to know that I do not care that you are a smuggler or a pirate or whatever people say you are," she said quietly. "Men must make their living somehow and you are making yours. Perhaps it is not the most honorable profession, but at least you are not a thief or a beggar. It could be worse."

He smiled, but it was without humor. "You may as well know all of it so there are no illusions of grandeur," he said. "I gamble. I own gambling establishments. If there is a money-making venture to be had, I usually participate. I am not a saint, Miss Edith. You may as well know that now because I am quite certain your mother filled your head with the rumors that abound about me, rumors that are more than likely true. But my character is not all damage and ruin. I have my good points. I am loyal to the bone. I would kill or die for my family and friends. And I never, ever lie. My word is my bond."

Edie smiled, but hers was genuine. "I find that all rather exciting," she said. "Perhaps it would bother some, but it does not bother me."

"You *do* understand that Polite Society does not speak fondly of me."

"Nor do they speak fondly of me," Edie said, her smile fading. "At least, that used to be the case. You already know that I was in love with another man. *Was.* He was married and I did not care, so you probably suspect that I am not a saint, either. I have not made wise choices in my life and I suppose that was what my mother was fearful of when we left the ball. Another questionable choice."

"With me?"

"With you."

"She would not have been wrong."

But Edie shook her head. "You come from a fine family, Rory, and your grandfather can smooth over any imperfections you may have," she said. "You will find a wife that is worthy of the grandson of a duke, but do not have any false impressions that I would be such a candidate."

"Why not?"

Those words hung in the air between them. Suddenly, his goal was revealed. The very reason for his presence was now laid bare and, for a moment, they looked at one another in shock – Rory because he'd said it and Edie because she'd heard it.

There was romance in the air.

"Can this be true?" Edie finally breathed. "Did you truly come with such intentions?"

Rory almost shook his head, as if he'd misspoken, but he couldn't bring himself to do it. Indeed, he'd come with such intentions. His attraction to Edie had been so strong from the beginning that he'd never entertained anything else. This beautiful, intelligent woman who found his lifestyle and reputation exciting.

Exciting!

God, maybe there *was* a woman meant just for him and her name was Edie Rhodes.

"I did," he said. "Miss Edith… Edie… may I call you Edie? I don't know why I ask because that is what I am going to call you whether or not you approve. I am a greatly flawed man, but you don't seem to mind. Am I misunderstanding you?"

Edie shook her head, but she was becoming edgy. Uncertain, even. Rory had appeared and declared his intentions and she simply didn't know what to make of it. It was all happening so quickly but, in the same breath, nothing had ever felt so right. With Myles, everything had been an uphill battle and, truth be told, she'd never felt her path with him was clear. She'd never felt that it was the right thing because she'd constantly had to fight for it.

But with Rory…

She wasn't fighting.

Everything was happening intuitively and easily.

God, maybe there *was* a man meant just for her and his name was Rory Flynn.

Except for one thing.

"No," she said, feeling her throat tighten with emotion. "You are not misunderstanding me. Perhaps you think I am a foolish creature because last night I was declaring my love for another man, but as you pointed out, it was not love. I am stubborn – terribly stubborn – so perhaps it was more a matter of refusing to surrender something I wanted. *Thought* I wanted. In any case, it was stupid of me. But what I said earlier is true – I am not meant for you, Rory. You must have someone virtuous and…"

He cut her off. "Virtuous?" he repeated. "Are you mad? You are the most virtuous woman. I *know* you are. You are from a good family with a mother who clearly watches out for you. How could I find someone more virtuous than you?"

Edie was willing to be truthful with him only so far. She simply couldn't confess her darkest sin to a man who thought she was pure and virtuous. Perhaps he was a gambler and a rake of the worst sort, but for a man, that could be acceptable to a certain extent, at least by some. A man could redeem himself in the eyes of the *ton*, but a woman… if Rory married her, it would do little to help his reputation. The poor man didn't need any assistance from her to be even more scorned than he already was.

It was a heartbreaking realization.

Unable to reply, the tears came before she could stop them. Humiliated that she'd started to cry, Edie whirled on her heel and ran off, dashing inside the garden gate and fleeing back to the house. Concerned, Rory followed her to the gate but would go no further. In fact, he sank back against the mews, watching her disappear into the house.

Baffled, he shook his head.

"What did I say?" he muttered to himself.

But it wasn't just to himself. Matilda was still standing there, watching. She'd been watching and listening to everything said. She may have been young, but she knew her sister well. She understood things that no one thought she was old enough to understand.

And she wasn't as naïve as her parents assumed.

"You called her virtuous," she said softly.

Rory looked at her, surprised. "You heard that?"

"I did."

"But why should that upset her so?"

Matilda gazed up at him with her big, dark eyes. "She wants to be," she said. "But Edie… she loved Myles. He promised her that he would divorce his wife and marry her. He told her that quite a lot. Edie used to write him letters every night and send them out with the maid to a tavern in town where Myles had a man who lived there, just to take her messages to him."

Rory had known about Forrester. But what he didn't know was how deeply involved Edie had been with him.

"I see," he said. "How long was this going on?"

"Two years," Matilda said. "But Myles was a friend of my father's, so she has known him a long time. We all have."

Rory digested that bit of information. "She told me about him," he said. "She told me that he lied to her."

Matilda nodded sadly. "My parents think I don't know what happened," she said. "But I know. Edie and I share a bedroom. I know everything that happens with her. I know she believed him when he told her that he loved her. I know she believed him when he told her that he would leave his wife and marry her. One night, he sent her a message asking her to meet him at The Hungry Horse."

"What's that?"

"A tavern near our home," Matilda said quietly. "She slipped out one night and met him there. One of the maids saw her go and followed her. She saw Myles and Edie go into the livery behind the tavern and then come out a short time later. She threatened to tell everyone but my father gave her money and sent her away. She still told people what she knew."

"And your sister knows this?"

Matilda shook her head. "Papa never told her," she said. "I only knew because I heard my parents arguing about it. It threatened to be a terrible scandal so Edie was restricted for at least two years, watched constantly, chaperoned everywhere, until Mama felt the scandal had faded. Until her friends no longer asked about it and went on to other gossip. But Edie… she does not feel as though she's virtuous because of it when the truth was that she only kissed Myles. There was nothing more."

"She told you that?"

"She did."

Rory thought on the truth of the matter, the shame that Edie had been forced to endure as the result of one ill-advised decision. His head turned in the direction of the house as if he could see Edie through the walls, realizing why she'd run from him. Why she'd told him he needed to find a virtuous wife. And then, stupidly, he'd called her virtuous when she knew damned well that she wasn't. She may have been honest with him about many things, but the one thing she'd hidden from him – her scandalous meeting with Forrester in a livery – remained buried.

A shame her parents had struggled to put behind her.

"Now I understand," he said, a hand to his forehead as he tried to think his way through this. "That's why she told me that she wasn't meant for me."

Matilda nodded. "Please don't tell her that I told you," she said, her eyes starting to well. "I love my sister. She is good and kind. But she believed Myles when he told her that he loved her. You cannot become angry that she believed him, can you?"

Rory looked at the girl, seeing the emotion. "Of course not," he said, reaching out to take her hand. "I am not angry at all, at least not with her. Now all of this makes so much sense."

Matilda nodded. "She was so afraid it would ruin her," she said. "It is difficult to be in love with a man who lies to you. My parents treated her like a prisoner for the past two years. This was supposed to be the Season that she entered into Polite Society again and then she met you."

He eyed her. "And your parents told her I would be her ruin just like Myles was, I would imagine."

"I'm sure my mother did."

Rory couldn't help but feel the disgust building in his chest. A beautiful woman who had been manipulated by a silver-tongued lover suffered the additional blow of being hidden away by her parents when the potentially devastating scandal surfaced. Not that he didn't understand why they did it, because he did. Her parents had been forced to take steps to salvage her reputation. It certainly wasn't the first time something like that had happened and Edie certainly wouldn't be the last girl it happened to, but it was a tragedy all around.

Still… Rory considered her virtuous. Compared to the women he knew, she was a veritable saint. He thought her father should know that in this world, someone thought Edie was wonderful and honorable.

Even if that someone was Rory Flynn.

"Miss Matilda," he said after a moment. "Where is your father?"

Matilda pointed to the house. "Inside."

"Will you take me to him?"

Matilda hesitated. Realizing he'd put her in an awkward position, at least in the eyes of her parents, for letting Rory Flynn in the house, he apologized. But he also thanked her.

A few moments with Matilda had made all the difference when it came to Edie.

Leaving the mews, Rory headed around to the front of the house and knocked firmly on the front door.

Frederick Rhodes was in for a big surprise.

CHAPTER ELEVEN

*"Thou shalt not be denied by anyone. Anyone who wants
to live a long and healthy life, that is."*
Sin Commandment #11

"I STILL HAVE business in London," Frederick said. "If you want to go home and take the children, that is your decision, but I must remain for the time being."

In the study of Rossington House, Henrietta stood in front of her husband's desk, wringing her hands with worry.

"Then we will go," Henrietta said. "Last night was a disaster in the making, Frederick. First the contact with Rory Flynn and then the appearance of Myles. I am seriously considering disallowing Edie to attend any further balls or social events. All she seems to do is attract the worst kind of man and we must protect Tilly."

Frederick sighed heavily. His wife was a good woman, but she could be extreme at times. "If we disallow Edie to attend anything social, where is she to find a husband?" he asked. "She must find one somewhere, Henny."

"Then you find her a husband," Henrietta implored. "She

cannot do it on her own. She hasn't the judgment you have."

Frederick didn't want to argue about his firstborn. He put up a hand to silence his wife. "I will think on it," he said. "It would not be fair to Edie to treat her like a prisoner, however."

"What do you mean a prisoner?" Henrietta said, incensed. "She is *not* a prisoner."

"Maybe not, but you are preparing to isolate her. Don't you think that's a bit severe?"

Henrietta appeared uncertain. "For her own protection."

"Is it?"

Before Henrietta could reply, they heard voices in the front of the house. Since Frederick's study was near the front door, he could hear something that sounded like an argument. He could hear his butler raising his voice to someone. Frederick looked at Henrietta curiously, as if she knew more than he did, but she simply shook her head. She was as puzzled as he was.

"*Stop, sir!*"

It was Frederick's butler. As Frederick rose to his feet, his curiosity turning to concern, a man he didn't recognize suddenly appeared in the doorway of the study.

"Lord Rossington, my name is Rory Flynn."

As Henrietta gasped, Frederick came around the side of his desk, looking at Rory with genuine bewilderment. Considering they'd just been speaking on the man, his appearance was as surprising as it was unexpected.

… or was it?

"Mr. Flynn," he said steadily. "I've heard the name."

Rory nodded, eyeing Lady Rossington as he entered. "I am certain that you have," he said. "My grandfather is the Duke of Savernake. I've come on a most personal matter, my lord. I beg only a moment of your time."

Henrietta looked at her husband in a panic, but Frederick seemed most interested in the appearance of the very man they'd been speaking of. Unlike his wife, he seemed to have a little more tolerance.

"This is most irregular," he said. "We've not formally met, though I know your grandfather."

"I realize that, my lord," Rory said. "But this is quite important. I would say critical in nature, even. It will only take a moment."

"I am afraid I am busy at this time," Frederick said. "Perhaps later…"

"It cannot wait, my lord. I am sorry." When Frederick opened his mouth to protest, Rory held up a hand. "I realize that I am an uninvited guest, but if you will only give me a moment of your time, I will make sure my grandfather knows that you were most generous and accommodating."

He was invoking his grandfather's name and for good reason. Of course Frederick should want the Duke of Savernake to know that he'd been kind to a wayward grandson. That would make him at least tolerant in the old man's eyes. Perhaps even forgivable since Henrietta had fled the ball the night before without so much as a farewell.

Therefore, his protests died.

Frederick could see the tall, dark, and handsome young man before him. He knew the rumors; everyone of import in London and perhaps even England did. The Sinning Flynns had been notorious for years. He'd heard the story of the previous evening from his wife, though she tended to dramatize things, and he'd not yet spoken to his daughter. Now, the very man at the center of the controversy had appeared at his home, which made the situation even more mysterious.

He *was* curious.

"Out of respect for your grandfather, you may proceed," he said. "But make it brief. What is your concern?"

Rory took a deep breath. "Your daughter," he said. "Edith. My lord, there seems to be an issue that I wish to discuss. It has come to my attention that Edith and the rest of your family left the Stag Ball last evening because of me. I have come to take issue with that and declare that nothing untoward happened between your daughter and me. In fact, just the opposite. I saved her."

Frederick's brow furrowed. "Saved her from what?"

"A man named Myles Forrester."

Henrietta gasped again and Frederick's brow furrowed with concern. "Forrester?" he said quite unhappily. "I was not aware that Edie had any contact with him last night."

"She did, my lord. I witnessed it."

"What happened?"

Rory couldn't help but notice the man had not asked him to sit down, which wasn't surprising considering he'd barged in uninvited. It was an utter breach of protocol and he knew it. But the subject was extremely important to him and he suspected he only had a few minutes before the viscount would chase him away.

Therefore, he spoke quickly and to the point.

"I found your daughter in the garden with the man," he said. "I do believe Edie was telling him she no longer wanted to see him again but he would not listen. Another man came upon them and assaulted Forrester. I pulled Edie away and hid her so that your family would be protected from any involvement in a common brawl at the Stag Ball. Such a thing would have been… scandalous. For your daughter's involvement, your family would have been banned from future gatherings, at the very least."

Frederick was still in shock at what he'd been told. "But my wife saw Forrester at the ball," he said. "Was he not banned for his involvement?"

Rory shrugged. "I do not know, but I suspect he will never return," he said. "Perhaps the decision was made not to remove him for fear of causing a scene. In any case, I had a glorious conversation with your daughter. I discovered her to be kind and bright and compassionate. Her impression on me was lasting, my lord, and if that is any indication what kind of woman she is, I suspect glorious is just the beginning. It is an impression that will last a lifetime."

Frederick wasn't quite sure what to say. "I will thank you for your kind words," he said. "But it was imperative you tell me this?"

Rory shook his head. "Not that," he said. "I was prefacing what I am about to say. My lord, I realize my reputation isn't as perfect as it should be. It is not perfect at all. I live my life the way I want to live it and you should know that I have no regrets except for in this moment. I was told that your wife removed your family from the ball after I invited them to the garden party at my father's home and that your wife did not wish for your family, and more specifically Edie, to be associated with me. Under normal circumstances, I would not take issue with this but, in this case, I must."

Frederick was looking the least bit uncomfortable. "So you've come to scold us?"

"No," Rory said. "I've come to tell you that in spite of my reputation and my dealings, the core of my soul is loyalty to my family and friends. I would kill or die for them. I may not have many virtues, but those that I do have are true. I am a responsible man. I am also an honest one. Perhaps those are qualities you would consider over everything else you've heard because I would like to court your daughter. As the grandson of a duke, I would ask for the consideration."

Henrietta had to put her hand over her mouth so she didn't speak out, a gut response to something she considered unsuitable and horrific. But her place in the home was not as the decision maker. That role was Frederick's. Her eyes went to him, wide and beseeching, but he wasn't looking at her.

He was looking at Rory.

"It seems to me that this is a discussion that must be given more time and thought than I have to give at the moment," he said. "As you said, you have come into my home, uninvited. I have given you time to state whatever it was that compelled you to do so. But when speaking of my daughter and her future, we must go through appropriate channels."

Rory wasn't sure what that meant. This entire situation was uncharted territory for him. "Are you saying that I am invited to return at another time?" he asked.

Frederick didn't reply right away. It was clear that he was thinking it over.

"I will speak with your grandfather first," he said. "At this time, I will not have this conversation with you."

That wasn't good enough for Rory. From what he had just heard, he had a suspicion that he would be cast aside and Edie would end up in a convent somewhere.

It was just a hunch he had.

"Forgive me, my lord," he said. "I have never done things the way they should be done, but a bold man takes risks and, in this case, I must be bold. I must tell you that Edie's failings mean far less to me than they do to you."

Frederick frowned. "What failings?"

Rory fixed on him. "I know of the scandal in the livery," he said, lowering his voice. "I know of her clandestine meeting with Forrester. I know that you are trying to reintroduce her back into Polite Society and keep this part of her past buried, but it seems to me that she is not being given a fair chance in any of this. The moment she met a man whose reputation is questionable, she was whisked away like a naughty child who should be punished."

Frederick stiffened. "Mr. Flynn, I fail to see…"

"It matters," Rory said, cutting him off perhaps a bit too sharply so he forced himself to calm. "I, myself, am a man with faults. That is difficult to admit for a Flynn, but I have my faults. Loyalty, compassion, and the love for my family have never been any of them, however. I understand that Edie was manipulated. She made a mistake. In many ways, she is as flawed as I am, but she is also far more perfect. I only ask that you consider allowing me to court her because you will not find anyone more willing to devote his time and his life to her."

"But…"

Rory wouldn't let him finish. "What if the man you are trying to match her with asks about the livery rumors?" he asked. "Will you tell him the truth? Or will you lie and say that it was nothing at all? If you seek to lie about it, then you will be establishing a relationship for Edie based on a lie. And what if he finds out that you have, in fact, lied to him? Lies never remain buried, my lord. They always surface."

Frederick looked at him, uncomfortable, realizing that Rory had figured out their entire scheme. "Until you find yourself in this position, Mr. Flynn," he said, "with a daughter who chose poorly, you will not understand the lengths a parent will go to in order to save a child."

Rory snorted softly. "My lord, I know what lengths a parent will go through," he said. "I have been watching my parents deal with scandal my entire life. But consider this – how do you think your lies will affect your younger daughter? If your deception is discovered, she will be ruined. I am telling you now that I know of Edie's past and it does not matter to me. Give me this opportunity to make her happy and you will not regret it, I swear it."

It was an impassioned plea. By the time he was finished, Frederick wasn't looking so shocked or so uncomfortable. In fact, he glanced at his wife as he turned away, making his way over to a sideboard that held fine imported brandy.

"Henrietta," he said quietly. "Leave us, my dear."

Henrietta was terribly reluctant. "But you cannot…"

"*Leave*. Please."

She couldn't argue with him. Slipping out of the study, she shut the door as Frederick busied himself at the sideboard. When he turned around, it was with two small crystal glasses of sherry.

"Here," he said. "I think you need this more than I do."

Hesitantly, Rory took the glass and downed the contents in one gulp. The liquid burned down his throat, but Rossington was right. He needed it.

"I did not mean to speak disrespectfully, my lord," he said. "Merely honestly. You view your daughter as a shame and I view her as a salvation."

Frederick glanced at him as he took a seat. "Yours?"

"Mine."

"But shouldn't salvation come from within?"

"Sometimes it needs a catalyst."

"True," Frederick said. His gaze lingered on Rory for a moment. "If it helps, I do not doubt your sincerity. I can see that you mean what you've said. But a man who has lived a life as you have lived yours… sometimes it is difficult to change."

"Not always, my lord," Rory said. "I've never had a reason to change."

"And you feel that Edie is that reason?"

"Will you at least let me prove it to you?"

"How?"

Rory didn't ask for permission for more sherry. He simply went to the table and poured himself more.

"You do understand that my wealth is greater than anyone in my family, including my grandfather?" he said.

Frederick shook his head. "I don't know that much about you other than your womanizing and gambling reputation."

Rory downed the sherry. "Your daughter would live like a queen," he said, smacking his lips. "There is nothing I cannot buy her. Nothing I would not give her were she to become my wife."

"But the gambling and womanizing?"

"Merely something to fill the emptiness, I suppose," Rory said. "I had no reason not to gamble or spend time with questionable women."

"And you think you can give all that up, just like that?"

"May I ask you a question, my lord?"

"What is it?"

"Did you have women before you married Lady Rossington?"

Frederick prepared to tell him that it was none of his affair, but he stopped short. He ended up snorting, handing his glass to Rory, who filled it for him and handed it back.

"All men have women before they marry," he muttered. "I was no different. If you want to know the truth, I did not live like a saint."

"Then you understand my position."

Frederick sipped his sherry as Rory pounded down another glass. "I understand what it is to be a young man who lives as he chooses," he said. "But if you truly wish to court my daughter, that will end."

"It will."

"Because of your eloquence when presenting your case, I am willing to overlook much of your reputation and even defend you if necessary, but not if you break your word to me."

"I am a man of my word, Lord Rossington."

Frederick merely acknowledged that he understood him, not that he believed him. He took another sip of sherry.

"The truth is that as much as Polite Society likes to turn their noses up at men like you, I can promise you that most of the men who comprise that group have lived freely and wildly at some point in their lives," he said. "The *ton* is full of hypocrites, Mr. Flynn. They love to point fingers and whisper about those who live their lives in a less conventional way while all the time, the men have mistresses and the women have affairs. They're just not as bold about it as you are."

Rory could see, in that instant, that Frederick had the capacity for understanding a man like him. He was right about the *ton* – they were hypocrites. They knew it and everyone else knew it but, still, they judged people.

It was simply the way of things.

"They have been weighing and measuring me since the day I was born," he said quietly. "They weighed and measured my father and tore my mother apart when she married him. Shall I tell you something?"

"Please do."

Drink in hand, Rory moved for a stiff, leather-bound chair. "Last night, I was going to seek revenge upon a man who had been speaking ill of my mother since she broke her engagement with him to marry my father," he said. "I was going to seduce one of his daughters and compromise her, humiliating the entire family. That was the plan, anyway. I will still seek revenge, though it will not be through seduction. Not if you allow me to court your daughter. But the point is that I defend those I love and punish those who hurt them. If you permit me, your daughter will fall into that category, too. I will defend her to the death, Lord Rossington. All other women will cease to exist for me."

"Nothing like a reformed rogue, as it were?"

"Rogues are rogues for a reason, usually," Rory said. "They are lacking something. They are trying to fill or find something. Sometimes they don't know what they need or want, but when they find it… knowing how hard it was to find that peace, they make for good husbands."

Frederick could see the passion, the determination. This was no flighty, ridiculous young man who behaved horribly and didn't care about the consequences. This was a deliberate and intense man, mature and wise beyond his years, who fought for what he believed in.

Frederick could see it in everything about him.

But that brought up something in his mind, a very salient point.

He had an idea.

"A few minutes ago, I asked you to prove your sincerity," he said. "Are you willing to do that?"

"I will do whatever you ask."

That was a terrifying amount of power given who had spoken the words. This was Rory Flynn, a man with a wicked reputation. He could do whatever he said he would do. Frederick inspected his glass for a moment, thoughtfully, before speaking.

"You said you were prepared to seek revenge last night over a man who wronged your mother," he said. Then his eyes flicked up to Rory. "Would you be prepared to do the same against a man who wronged Edie?"

The light of understanding flickered in Rory's eyes. "Let me guess," he said. "Forrester?"

"For what he has done, he deserves no less."

The corners of Rory's mouth twitched with a smile. "I would do this and gladly," he said. "What would you have me do?"

"I do not want to see him again," Frederick said. "Make it so that he never shows himself to Edie again. Ever. The man has done unfathomable damage and I want him to pay. If you feel for her as you say you do, then you will want that, also."

"With pleasure, my lord."

"Return to me when the deed is done and I will let you court my daughter."

Rory didn't have to be asked twice.

CHAPTER TWELVE

*"There comes a time in every man's life when roads lead
to different destinations. Be sure not to choose the road
to ruin."*

Sin Commandment #12

S HE'D HEARD HIM come in the house.

Edie had been standing on the stair landing leading
from the first to the second floor, the one with the enormous
window that overlooked the garden and the mews. On sunny
days, it was like a picture window into heaven because of the
vibrant sky against the lush and colorful garden, but she'd been
standing at the window in tears, not quite ready to run to her
bedroom and shut the door but also not quite ready to return to
Rory and apologize for her behavior.

She simply couldn't help it.

He'd struck a chord with her in calling her virtuous. She
could have taken any other word – lovely, kind, or even silly –
but virtuous had sent her fleeing. Because she knew that she
wasn't virtuous and he didn't. He didn't know anything about
her.

He was attracted to an illusion.

An illusion of her parents' creation.

Her parents had tried very hard to present her as a normal, honorable young lady after the events of two years ago. It was a dark period in her past that would remain dark and buried as her parents tried to convince the *ton* that the eldest daughter of Viscount Rossington was an eligible marital prospect by bringing her to the Stag Ball.

Every eligible young woman at the ball was looking for a husband and Edie had been no exception, at least in the eyes of the *ton*. They whispered about her – she knew that – but because her father had an excellent reputation and the family in general was well respected, Edie wasn't shunned. She was still whispered about, but she wasn't shunned.

She was an illusion.

She'd been honest with Rory about everything else so it was probably best if she was honest about this, too. If Rory was appalled and talked about it, then her chances of a good marriage were gone. Even if the news was coming from a Sinning Flynn, it would be believed. She was taking a great chance in telling him that, but for her own sake, she felt she had to. Her parents had tried so hard to bury a scandal that she was about to openly admit.

She had been standing on the landing, trying to summon the courage, when she saw Rory depart and Matilda head into the house.

Greatly curious, she went downstairs, trying to catch a glimpse of Rory through the widows facing the side avenue. Rossington House was right on a corner, so she could see people and carriages passing by. She could also see Rory. She followed him right up until he ended up on the main avenue and she though that would be her last look at him.

But it wasn't.

Rory went right to the front door and pounded.

Her father's butler, a big man with a deep voice, answered. As Edie cowered around a corner, trying to hear what was said, she could hear Rory's voice and the butler's voice, but not the actual words. Those came a few seconds later when voices were raised and Rory demanded to see Lord Rossington.

Rory finally pushed past the butler and went straight into her father's study.

Startled, Edie tried to hear what was being said but they were too far away. When the door shut and the butler was finally sent away in a flustered mess, Edie slipped closer until she was able to get near the door.

And what she heard shocked her to the bone.

So much came out in that brief conversation between Rory and her father, not the least of which was the fact that Rory knew about the scandal in the livery at The Hungry Horse. Edie had no idea how he could know such a thing, *truly* know such a thing, and she resisted the urge to run and hide until she heard more.

But Rory didn't seem to care about any of that.

He wanted to court her.

Overwhelmed with what she was hearing, Edie had to scrambled to hide when Henrietta was asked to leave. The study door opened and slammed shut with her mother scurrying away with as much frustration as the butler had. Rory seemed to have that effect on them. Once her mother walked away, heading up the stairs, Edie returned to her position with her ear against the door, but the voices were so low that she couldn't hear much more. The removal of her mother had the men speaking in softer tones and, anxious, she moved away from the door and went to sit near the door leading to the garden, a sunny corner that her mother sometimes used for her sewing but with a clear view of the study door.

And she waited.

It was less than an hour when Rory finally emerged from her father's study and headed for the rear door. He would have walked right past Edie had she not called out to him, quietly.

"Rory?"

He froze, turning in the direction of the voice and spying her through the doorway of the small room. She was sitting at the window, illuminated by the light that danced around her like a halo. He quickly moved in her direction as she stood up from the seat.

"I was contemplating apologizing to you for my silly behavior when I heard you knock at the door," she said before he could speak. "I will not ask you what you said to my father, but I wanted to tell you that I am sorry I ran from you. It was inexcusable."

Rory smiled faintly. "I hardly noticed," he said. "Perhaps you had something very important to tend to inside and you did not have time to tell me."

It was her turn to smile. "You are kind," she said. "But, then again, you have been kind since I met you. For two people who met by chance and have yet to be formally introduced, I would say that we have had more than our share of interaction."

Rory couldn't disagree. He indicated for her to regain her seat at the window bench as he pulled up a small chair against the wall.

"Even if you will not ask me what business I had with your father, I will tell you," he said. "The business had to do with you."

She nodded faintly. "I know," she said. "Although I told you that I will not ask you what your business was with my father, the truth is that I heard some of it. May I ask a question?"

"Certainly."

"Who told you?"

"Told me what?"

"About me. Who told you?"

Rory understood. "It wasn't rumor or gossip if that is what you mean," he said, thinking she seemed quite calm about such an explosive subject. "It was a reliable source, told to me in the strictest confidence. I will never repeat it. Are you angry?"

Edie shook her head. "No," she said, leaning back against the wall in a resigned gesture. "In fact, I had made the decision to tell you myself before I heard what you and my father were discussing. I cannot imagine what impression I ever made on you that you would want to court me, even after knowing everything. It would not be fair to you not to tell you."

He folded his arms across his broad chest, leaning against the wall behind him, adopting a casual stance because she was. Though Edie's manner seemed to suggest defeat more than anything, Rory wasn't going to give in to it.

He'd never been more elated about anything in his life.

This flawed woman who might actually accept his suit.

"If you know half the things about me that are said, then you know I am in no position to judge," he said. "I look at you and I don't see a fallen woman or whatever your parents would have you believe. You're not fallen, Edie. And you're still virtuous to me."

"How can you even say that?"

"Virtue means many things but, in this case, it means honor," he said. "You were going to tell me of your deepest secret yourself which means you are a woman of honor. That kind of honor and honesty must be respected and celebrated."

"What do you mean?"

He shrugged, averting his gaze. But he ended up looking at her hands. She had such lovely hands. Covered by the gloves the previous night, he'd never noticed.

"I have spent my entire life trying to satisfy something within me that I simply couldn't satisfy," he said. "Not money nor women nor gambling could satisfy me. I feel as if I've spent my entire life searching for something that would bring me happiness but I never knew what that was until I met you. An honest and vulnerable woman who is like me in many ways. Does it seem strange for me to say that?"

Edie had heard him speaking to her father, so she wasn't completely surprised by his declaration, but even so, hearing it from his lips brought her a sense of awe.

"Yes," she said honestly. "Because I've never had anyone say such things to me. How can you possibly know such things about me? We've only spoken a few times. You have seen me at my very worst. How can you know I am someone you would like to court?"

He unfolded his arms and sat forward, closer to her. "If you have grace and dignity at your worst, imagine what you will have at your best," he said, his eyes glimmering warmly. "Edie… I cannot tell you what has drawn me to you, only that something has. Something great and glorious. Meeting you made me forget a life that I thought was set, a path that I thought was clear."

"What path was that?"

He debated about telling her. But since she had been honest

with him, he thought it only right to be honest with her. He'd told her father, after all.

Perhaps it was time to start trusting people a little.

"I was at the Stag Ball last night because I had sworn revenge upon a man who has slandered my mother for years," he said. "I told you that I have a strong sense of loyalty to my family. I suppose it is the Irish in me. But I attended the ball with the sole purpose of seeking this man, and his daughters, and making sure they left the ball in humiliation. I'd been waiting years for this, Edie, and last night was my chance. But I met you and it was as if the moon and stars aligned somehow. Though I've not forgotten my vow, you had my attention, all of it, from nearly the moment I met you. Needless to say, my plans for revenge did not come to fruition."

Edie was serious as she looked at him. "But why revenge?" she said. "Why must you do this?"

"Because it is time the Flynns fought for their honor a little," he said, sounding grim. "The man I speak of was once my mother's betrothed. When my mother left him for my father, this man spoke ill of my mother and continued to do so for years. His own brother was my instructor at Oxford and the brother spent a good deal of time humiliating me in front of my peers. It was time for me to pay them back for so much hurt and shame."

"Oxford," she repeated. "I did not know you attended Oxford."

He smiled faintly. "There is much you do not know about me," he said. "All I ask is that you give me the chance to teach you."

The expression on her face was full of hope, something she'd not had in a very long time.

"Are you *certain*?" she asked softly.

He nodded, moving his chair closer to her. "Very much," he said. "You make me want to be a better man, Edie. I've never wanted that before. I've never cared."

Edie gazed back at him, feeling a myriad of emotions. The last time she'd had a man this close to her, it was Myles as he lied to her yet again. She could always tell when he was lying to her, or trying to, because he began to tremble. His voice trembled. She used to find it endearing but as she listened to Rory's impassioned plea, she realized that it had all been ridiculous and tiresome. Rory had been correct; she hadn't loved Myles. She had been in love with the idea of love and nothing more. She hadn't known the difference.

Until now.

Now, gazing into Rory's handsome face, she could see so many possibilities. She could see a man who understood her sins and forgave them. She could see a man who was imperfect but who wanted to do better.

And he wanted to do it with her by his side.

It was difficult to know how people fell in love. Sometimes it took years. Sometimes days. Sometimes hours. It was simply a matter of knowing when the situation and the person were right. A man with so many flaws understood flaws. He understood her failings. Edie knew, as long as she lived, that she could never ask for anything better. As he reached out to take her fingers, she lifted both hands and gently cupped his face.

"Swear to me that this is what you truly want," she whispered.

Rory closed his eyes to her soft, gentle touch. "It is what I truly want."

"And swear to me that from this day forward, I will be the

only woman you ever think about."

"I swear it."

"The only woman you will ever love."

"I cannot swear that."

"*What?*"

His eyes opened, twinkling with humor. "I love my mother," he said. "And if we have a daughter, I will love her, also."

She fought off a grin. "Very well," she said. "You may love your mother and our girl children. But any other woman…"

"There will never *be* any other woman," he murmured. "Our path may not be easy, but it is our path and we will stay the course. We will fight for our right to be happy. I will never leave your side, Edie. Not even after the stars fall from the heavens and the moon is but ashes. Even then, I shall remain by your side, for always."

Edie believed him. There was nothing about the man that didn't scream sincerity and she believed him without question.

Without reserve.

Forever.

Reaching out, Rory put his arms around her, gently, and pulled her to him, slanting his mouth over hers and kissing her gently. She tasted so delicious that he pulled her closer, feasting on lips that belonged to him. Tasting the woman he would taste for the rest of his life. Her scent was intoxicating, filling his nostrils, making his heart race. That kiss, that moment, was seared into his brain.

For eternity.

When Frederick came out of his study a few minutes later, he happened to catch sight of Rory and Edie in an amorous embrace. They were lost in each other's arms and although Frederick should have separated them and thrown Rory into the street, he didn't have the heart to. Well did he remember what it was like to kiss the woman he was going to marry.

With a grin, he looked the other way and went about his business.

CHAPTER THIRTEEN

*"Like a fine wine, the taste of revenge changes as it
grows older…"*
Sin Commandment #13

The Pox Tavern
London

"Y OU TRACKED HIM here?" Rory asked.

Gabriel DeWolfe, an old friend, nodded grimly.
"Inside," he said. "You told me who you were looking for and I
put my men on it. Forrester wasn't difficult to find. The man
doesn't cover his tracks in the least."

Rory nodded, peering inside the dirty panes of glass, into
the most notorious tavern in all of London. The Pox had been
around for centuries, with different owners, but always the
same clientele – people with no names, or those who wanted to
forget, or those who simply wanted a good time with no
commitment. The bad, the ugly, and the incorrigible were
regular patrons. There were a thousand reasons for frequenting
a place like that and not one of them was honorable.

There was still gambling at The Pox, infamous for that

particular feature because a man could bet on anything and everything, making it a dangerous place, indeed. Rory had once tried to buy a stake in The Pox, but the risks were great. The current owner ran a ring of thugs who roughed up business owners and merchants near the River Thames who refused to pay a protection fee. As Rory had said many times, he was many things, but being an extortionist wasn't one of them.

Even a Flynn had his standards.

That didn't mean he didn't enjoy a game at The Pox now and again, which ran in direct competition with his own gambling enterprise, another ancient establishment called Gomorrah. Gomorrah was more of a combination gambling den and brothel while The Pox was everything else.

It was a wild place.

But they'd found Myles Forrester here.

"Where are your men now, Gabe?" he asked.

Gabriel, a tall and handsome man, tilted his head back towards the livery behind The Pox. "In the alley," he said. "They can move in and collect Forrester if you want them to. I wasn't sure if you wanted to do this yourself."

DeWolfe had a private security service, men hired by the wealthy for a variety of protection and security reasons, but Rory had called upon him for assistance with Myles Forrester, who was particularly squirrely.

It had been an interesting hunt.

After his encounter with Rossington, Rory had set off to find Forrester. That's when he called upon Gabriel, who did this kind of thing for a living. After the Stag Ball, Forrester had retreated to a London hotel he frequented and, as Rory found out, had tried to make contact with Edie by sending her a message through his valet. Edie had returned the message unopened, unaware that Rory had been tasked with removing Forrester from her life permanently, but that rejected message was enough to give Rory a direction.

Forrester was staying at Grenier's.

It was a fashionable hotel for the *ton*, but by the time Rory got there, Forrester had left and it had been a chase ever since. Frederick thought he might have even come to Rossington House to contact Edie directly because a servant recognized him on the street in front of the home, but he never came to the house. DeWolfe's men trailed him to The Pox, a seedy establishment for a man who was part of Polite Society, but it didn't matter why he was here, only that he was.

The hunt was over.

"I do not need to go into The Pox myself," Rory said after a moment of deliberation. "Have your men bring him out here. My men from Cornwall are across the way with a wagon. See them?"

He was pointing to the road that paralleled the river. There were at least five men standing around an old cart, filled with straw and barrels. There was also a coffin on the cart, a plain pine box, just waiting to be filled.

Gabriel could see it in the light of the torches.

"Is *that* what you intend to transport him in?" He grinned.

Rory showed little emotion. "I have been tasked with making sure the man never returns to London," he said. "Outright murder isn't something I would indulge in, so I will remove Forrester, who will more than likely wish I'd killed him before this is over with."

Gabriel was trying not to laugh. "What do you intend to do?"

"You'll see," Rory said with a glimmer in his eyes. "But

before I depart, I want to speak to you about something else I'll need your help with."

"What is that?"

"I've a score to settle with the Earl of Exford," Rory said. "As, it turns out, I can no longer settle it the way I'd intended. My plan was to ruin one of the daughters but, somehow, I don't think ruining an innocent woman's life is the way to go about it. My vengeance is against the father, not the daughters."

Gabriel looked at him curiously. "The Rory Flynn I've known for years would not care whose life he ruins."

"The Rory Flynn you've known for years has grown a conscience when it comes to innocent young women," Rory said, making a face as if such a thing was distasteful. "Do you know of anyone who can ruin the man financially?"

"Perhaps," Gabriel said. "What did you have in mind?"

Rory pondered the question for a moment. "I understand Exford likes to invest his money in speculations," he said. "I heard a rumor that he was interested in purchasing his own vineyard in Burgundy."

"Who told you that?"

"My grandfather's butler, of all people," Rory said. "He heard Exford talking about it at the Stag Ball. In fact, several people heard him talk about it. He made no secret of it, hoping that somehow it might attract a husband for his daughters. What man wouldn't want to marry into a family with its own vineyard?"

"Ah!" Gabriel was beginning to get the picture. "And you want someone to pose as a Burgundian willing to sell a vineyard?"

"Or a Flemish lord with ancient family vineyards looking to offload them because he needs the money."

Gabriel grinned. "I know exactly what you mean."

"Good," Rory said, satisfied that his plan for Exford would still come to completion even though it wasn't the way he had originally intended. But somehow, this way seemed more fulfilling. "Meanwhile… tell your men in the alley to bring Forrester to me."

Gabriel did.

The DeWolfe men entered from the alley, pushing into The Pox and cornering Forrester as he sat with two women he was plying with drink. That tremulous, little boy appeal was abruptly cut short when the men addressed him by name and he responded. Pushing the women aside, they lifted Forrester out of his seat and literally carried the man outside as he struggled and protested.

There, they were met by Rory's men from Cornwall, men who were part of his smuggling fleet. Pirates, some would call them. But they were mostly men of profit and adventure. Rory paid them extremely well for their loyalty and because of that, they would do anything for him.

Even kidnap someone.

They took Myles Forrester, happily.

Gabriel DeWolfe only heard what happened to Forrester quite some time later when he happened to run into Forbes Dinnington. As Forbes told it, Myles Forrester was taken all the way to Mousehole, Cornwall, confined to a coffin, where Rory anchored his fleet of seven fast and sleek ships. They were some of the fastest ships in the world and they had to be for the jobs they undertook. Myles was bundled up onto a ship that was heading for China.

A journey that took several months.

The last anyone saw of Myles Forrester was when he was

taken off the ship at Shanghai, put in a cage, and became part of a caravan heading for Mongolia. Some say he became a prisoner of the Qing dynasty. Others said he ended up becoming a servant in the house of a fine dowager. No one knew for sure. But the truth is that he never came back.

And that was the way Rory had planned it.

For Edie, he would have plucked the moon from the sky and given it to her had she asked for it, but sending the man who had tried to ruin her life into exile was a lot more satisfying.

When Frederick found out, he thought so, too.

EPILOGUE

"Sometimes, life brings the joy of surprising things."
Sin Commandments – last entry

Rossington House
One year later

"DO THESE THINGS always take so long?"

The question came from Rory as he sat in Frederick's study, nursing his fourth brandy of the afternoon and feeling the least bit woozy. But his wooziness wasn't only from the brandy.

The wait for his son was in full swing.

Frederick was sitting behind his desk, brandy within arm's reach. He grinned at his nervous son-in-law, a man he'd become quite fond of.

"My wife has given birth to two children," he said. "With Edie, it took two days, but with Tilly, it took an hour. At least, it felt that way. I suppose every woman is different."

"I suppose," Rory said. "But I've no experience with this kind of thing. How can you remain so calm?"

"Simple," Frederick said. "I drink my brandy and try not to

think about it. Shall we play cards to pass the time?"

Rory eyed him. "No," he said flatly. "I'll be distracted and you'll end up winning a fortune. But that was a nice try."

Frederick laughed softly and turned back to his drink as Rory found himself looking at the ceiling. Edie was up there. She'd been in labor with their first child for about eight hours, since the early morning. They'd been at Rossington House for the past few months because that was where Edie wanted their child to be born, in the very house where she'd been born. But mostly, she very much wanted the comfort of Rossington and the reputable midwives and doctors of London.

It had been Frederick who had paid for the very best midwife he could find, mostly because Edie didn't want a male doctor in her room with her legs spread, as she put it. Now came the waiting game, as Henrietta and Matilda were in the room with Edie while Rory quite gladly waited it out with Frederick, a man he'd become close to over the past year.

Unable to continue sitting, Rory stood up and began to pace.

"Hopefully, it will all be over soon and I shall be holding my son in my arms," he said. "And this midwife is the very best? The very best reputation?"

Frederick had answered that question about twenty times over the past few months. "The very best, I promise," he said. "If you do not believe me, go upstairs and see for yourself."

Rory shook his head. As a man, he was fearless, but as a husband and father, childbirth terrified him.

"I believe you," he said. "I promised my mother that I would send word to her the moment we knew. She wanted to come to London, you know, but she has been ill and my father would not allow her to travel."

Frederick nodded. "I know," he said. "But I look forward to seeing your parents again when they come to see the new baby."

Sean and Amy had been to London for the wedding of Rory and Edie about a year ago, shortly after the death of the Duke of Savernake, but they'd returned to Cornwall a few months later where Amy had contracted an illness in her chest. The death of her father had weakened her spirit and Sean was convinced that it had also affected her health, hence her inability to recover from something as common as a chest cold.

It was something Rory didn't like to think about.

Two deaths of two people he loved in a short amount of time was something he simply couldn't fathom.

The truth was that the death of his grandfather had left a hole in his heart. He was still grieving the man who had passed on just when he was coming to know him, but he was grateful that he'd had the chance to strengthen their relationship towards the end. There was no longer the disinterested disconnect between them but, in the duke's last days, their bond had grown into something more familial and warm. He only wished the duke had lived to see the birth of a great-grandchild.

It was his one regret.

As Rory sat there, musing about his grandfather, one of Rossington's footmen entered the study.

"Mr. Flynn," he said. "There is a man to see you in the mews."

Rory looked over his shoulder at him. "Who is it?"

"He says DeWolfe sent him."

That had Rory on his feet. He quickly made his way out of the house, through the verdant garden, and to the mews where, indeed, one of Gabriel's men was waiting for him. Rory recognized him as having been at The Pox all those months ago.

"You have a message for me?" Rory asked.

The man, older and somewhat grizzled, nodded as he motioned for Rory to follow him. Rory did, away from the mews and the servants who were working on Rossington's fine barouche.

"Well?" Rory said impatiently when they were far enough away. "What is it?"

The man turned to him. "Gabriel wanted me to tell you that, by tonight, it will be all over London that the Earl of Exford will have lost all of his money to a known swindler," he said quietly. "Exford is trying very hard to keep this news quiet, but we've already been whispering it to the servants of some of the most important people in London. By tonight, everyone will know."

Rory's eyebrows lifted. "Finally," he said, pleasure echoing in his voice. "The Scotsman finally came through, did he?"

The man nodded. "A criminal known as Gregor MacGregor convinced Exford to invest the majority of his money in a vineyard in the Loire Valley. He promised Exford that he'd be a rich man. But MacGregor is a known swindler. He gave Exford forged documents and maps, worked the deal, and the man fell right into the trap."

A smile tugged on Rory's lips. "He lost everything?"

The man nodded, seeing the delight in Rory's eyes. "Mostly everything," he said. "According to MacGregor, Exford just returned from France and the lands he does not own. He nearly started another war with France because the French count living on the lands took great offense to Exford attempting to evict him. The man made a damned fool out of himself. Once the news of his folly spreads, his shame will be endless."

Rory couldn't help the smile now. It was exactly what he

wanted to hear. Finally, his revenge against Exford had come to fruition and he couldn't have been more delighted. Better still, he didn't have to ruin an innocent woman's life to do it. Since his marriage to Edie, he was a kinder and gentler man, but that didn't extend to Exford. For all of those years the man tore down Amy, for all of the pain and strife he'd caused, now he was going to know the taste of humiliation and failure.

Rory couldn't have been happier about it.

"I can move the situation along," he said. "I will be delighted to tell Rossington about Exford's failure and I will also send a message to the new Duke of Savernake, Uncle Martin. The Savernake servants will spread the news more quickly than a spark on kindling. Exford will know shame as he's never known before when I am finished with him."

The man nodded in agreement. "Gabriel wants to know if you need anything else."

Rory shook his head. "Tell Gabriel that I am pleased," he said. "Quite pleased. In fact, tell him that I have one hundred bottles of the finest French claret with his name on them. I will have them delivered tomorrow."

The man grinned. "I will tell him."

As the man scurried back down the mews, Rory turned for the house. His vengeance was evidently satisfied, his wife was delivering his first child, and life as he knew it was better than it had ever been. Sometimes, he still couldn't believe it. That terrible rake known as Rory Flynn had found joy and comfort in something he never thought he would.

A wife and family.

He was still surprised to realize that.

He was halfway across the garden when Henrietta suddenly appeared in the garden door, waving frantically at him.

"Rory!" she called.

Rory saw her and bolted, rushing to the house faster than he'd ever moved in his life. "Well?" he demanded. "Is Edie in trouble?"

Henrietta smiled, which was a rare occurrence when it came to Rory. She'd had an entire year to become used to the man and saw, as everyone else did, that he was a sincere, compassionate, and loving husband and father. The transformation had been astonishing, something that softened even Henrietta's hardened heart.

But today was a day for rejoicing. Reaching out, she put a hand on his arm.

"No," she said. "Edie is quite well. The baby has arrived. You have a son, Rory. A fine son who looks just like Edie."

Rory didn't remember running from the garden all the way to the bedroom on the third floor, the one he shared with his wife. The very room she had been born in those years ago. What he did remember was the feeling when the midwife placed his son in his arms for the first time and he found himself looking at a baby that, he thought, looked more like him. He also remembered the feeling when he looked at his exhausted, smiling wife.

Joy.

Unmitigated joy.

Little Wellesbourne Sean Frederick Hugh Flynn, or Welles – Wellie to his mother – had a life ahead of him that he could have never imagined. Rory had it all planned out, but as he looked at that tiny face, all he could see was the culmination of dreams he never even knew he had. From the last Stag Ball where he'd planned to execute his vengeance to the bedside of his wife as he held their son in his arms, the reality that his life had become seemed like a fantasy to him. A fantasy that he would gladly indulge in for the rest of his life. Rory Flynn, the wildest Flynn brother of all, was wild no more.

But Welles grew up with his father's wild streak.

Another story for another time.

ෆ THE END ෨

Kathryn Le Veque Novels

Medieval Romance:

De Wolfe Pack Series:
Warwolfe
The Wolfe
Nighthawk
ShadowWolfe
DarkWolfe
A Joyous de Wolfe Christmas
BlackWolfe
Serpent
A Wolfe Among Dragons
Scorpion
StormWolfe
Dark Destroyer
The Lion of the North
Walls of Babylon
The Best Is Yet To Be
BattleWolfe
Castle of Bones

De Wolfe Pack Generations:
WolfeHeart
WolfeStrike
WolfeSword
WolfeBlade
WolfeLord
WolfeShield
Nevermore
WolfeAx

The Executioner Knights:
By the Unholy Hand
The Mountain Dark
Starless
A Time of End
Winter of Solace
Lord of the Sky
Splendid Hour
The Whispering Night
Netherworld
Lord of the Shadows
Of Mortal Fury

The de Russe Legacy:
The Falls of Erith
Lord of War: Black Angel
The Iron Knight
Beast
The Dark One: Dark Knight
The White Lord of Wellesbourne
Dark Moon
Dark Steel
A de Russe Christmas Miracle
Dark Warrior

The de Lohr Dynasty:
While Angels Slept
Rise of the Defender
Steelheart
Shadowmoor
Silversword
Spectre of the Sword
Unending Love
Archangel
A Blessed de Lohr Christmas

The Brothers de Lohr:
The Earl in Winter

Lords of East Anglia:
While Angels Slept
Godspeed
Age of Gods and Mortals

Great Lords of le Bec:
Great Protector

House of de Royans:
Lord of Winter
To the Lady Born
The Centurion

Lords of Eire:
Echoes of Ancient Dreams
Blacksword
The Darkland

Ancient Kings of Anglecynn:
The Whispering Night
Netherworld

Battle Lords of de Velt:
The Dark Lord
Devil's Dominion
Bay of Fear
The Dark Lord's First Christmas
The Dark Spawn
The Dark Conqueror
The Dark Angel

Reign of the House of de Winter:
Lespada
Swords and Shields

De Reyne Domination:
Guardian of Darkness
Black Storm

A Cold Wynter's Knight
With Dreams
Master of the Dawn

House of d'Vant:
Tender is the Knight (House of d'Vant)
The Red Fury (House of d'Vant)

The Dragonblade Series:
Fragments of Grace
Dragonblade
Island of Glass
The Savage Curtain
The Fallen One

Great Marcher Lords of de Lara
Dragonblade

House of St. Hever
Fragments of Grace
Island of Glass
Queen of Lost Stars

Lords of Pembury:
The Savage Curtain

Lords of Thunder: The de Shera Brotherhood Trilogy
The Thunder Lord
The Thunder Warrior
The Thunder Knight

The Great Knights of de Moray:
Shield of Kronos
The Gorgon

The House of De Nerra:
The Promise
The Falls of Erith
Vestiges of Valor

Realm of Angels

Highland Warriors of Munro:
The Red Lion
Deep Into Darkness

The House of de Garr:
Lord of Light
Realm of Angels

Saxon Lords of Hage:
The Crusader
Kingdom Come

High Warriors of Rohan:
High Warrior

The House of Ashbourne:
Upon a Midnight Dream

The House of D'Aurilliac:
Valiant Chaos

The House of De Dere:
Of Love and Legend

St. John and de Gare Clans:
The Warrior Poet

The House of de Bretagne:
The Questing

The House of Summerlin:
The Legend

The Kingdom of Hendocia:
Kingdom by the Sea

Regency Historical Romance:
Sin Like Flynn: A Regency
Historical Romance Duet

Gothic Regency Romance:
Emma

Contemporary Romance:

**Kathlyn Trent/Marcus Burton
Series:**
Valley of the Shadow
The Eden Factor
Canyon of the Sphinx

**The American Heroes Anthology
Series:**
The Lucius Robe
Fires of Autumn
Evenshade
Sea of Dreams
Purgatory

**Other non-connected
Contemporary Romance:**
Lady of Heaven
Darkling, I Listen
In the Dreaming Hour
River's End
The Fountain

Sons of Poseidon:
The Immortal Sea

**Pirates of Britannia Series (with
Eliza Knight):**
Savage of the Sea by Eliza Knight
Leader of Titans by Kathryn Le
Veque
The Sea Devil by Eliza Knight
Sea Wolfe by Kathryn Le Veque

Note: All Kathryn's novels are designed to be read as stand-alones, although many have cross-over characters or cross-over family groups. Novels that are grouped together have related characters or family groups. You will notice that some series have the same books; that is because they are cross-overs. A hero in one book may be the secondary character in another.

There is NO reading order except by chronology, but even in that case, you can still read the books as stand-alones. No novel is connected to another by a cliff hanger, and every book has an HEA.

Series are clearly marked. All series contain the same characters or family groups except the American Heroes Series, which is an anthology with unrelated characters.

For more information, find it in **A Reader's Guide to the Medieval World of Le Veque**.

ABOUT KATHRYN LE VEQUE

Bringing the Medieval to Romance

KATHRYN LE VEQUE is a critically acclaimed, multiple USA TODAY Bestselling author, an Indie Reader bestseller, a charter Amazon All-Star author, and a #1 bestselling, award-winning, multi-published author in Medieval Historical Romance with over 100 published novels.

Kathryn is a multiple award nominee and winner, including the winner of Uncaged Book Reviews Magazine 2017 and 2018 "Raven Award" for Favorite Medieval Romance. Kathryn is also a multiple RONE nominee (InD'Tale Magazine), holding a record for the number of nominations. In 2018, her novel WARWOLFE was the winner in the Romance category of the Book Excellence Award and in 2019, her novel A WOLFE AMONG DRAGONS won the prestigious RONE award for best pre-16th century romance.

Kathryn is considered one of the top Indie authors in the world with over 2M copies in circulation, and her novels have been translated into several languages. Kathryn recently signed with Sourcebooks Casablanca for a Medieval Fight Club series, first published in 2020.

In addition to her own published works, Kathryn is also the President/CEO of Dragonblade Publishing, a boutique publishing house specializing in Historical Romance. Dragonblade's success has seen it rise in the ranks to become Amazon's #1 e-book publisher of Historical Romance (K-Lytics report July 2020).

Kathryn loves to hear from her readers. Please find Kathryn on Facebook at Kathryn Le Veque, Author, or join her on Twitter @kathrynleveque. Sign up for Kathryn's blog at www.kathrynleveque.com for the latest news and sales.